Aunt Cora's Wart

An Historical Faerie Tale

* * *

"Nipper Fest!"

by

Mary Groce

Dedication

*to Susan Atlas ("Grandma Butch"),
my muse and my naughty angel;
and to "Uncle" Christopher Andrew
Maier,
for opening our eyes to the
wonders of Camden*

*to Howard —
What a pleasure
to meet you!
Fly high —
Mary +

Guy*

6-23-18

Contents

*"The boundless vista
and the horizon far and dim
are all here."*

—Walt Whitman

1. A Peachy Gray Day

I open one eye. Only one. Diamonds glisten on the giant windowpane as the sun tries to greet me through the early morning rain (hey, I'm a poet!). I'm still half-way inside my dream of flying through the air like Peter Pan...or like my great-great-great Uncle Emory, who was the first licensed black pilot, and a barnstormer—a pioneer in aviation. He was so brave, flying his homemade gliders across the Susquehanna River to his job as a farmhand, and going way up in those old Curtiss pushers, which were like box kites with engines. If only I had known him...if only I could fly! At least I can in my dreams. I start to roll over, when I suddenly remember where I am...Grandma Butch and Buckadee's! I catch a whiff of buckwheat pancakes as I throw off my covers.

"Good Morning, Sunshine!" laughs Grandma Butch in her deep, musical voice. "How did you sleep? That sofa bed's usually pretty comfy."

"Like a log!" I answer as I walk over to the kitchen counter to watch her flip another flapjack. Except for the counter, the kitchen and living room of the apartment are really one big room—all gray and white and silver, with a hint of yellow and orange. The armless, legless mannequin that Grandma Butch rescued from a trash can is peering out from behind the sofa. Her name is Daphne, and she's decked out with steampunk goggles and a fancy silver striped scarf. Sometimes she wears a *chapeau,* but today she's gloriously bald. Daphne ignores me as I cross the room.

"Good! Breakfast will be ready in about two shakes, as soon as your Buckadee is done going over a couple of songs for the Nipper Fest this afternoon. She'll be transformed into Geraldine Farrar, wig and bling and all, in a few hours. Just wait till you see her—you won't recognize her! Oh Jenna, we're so glad you could visit us this weekend. Our Victor building with its Nipper Tower is celebrating its Centennial today!"

"Wow, a hundred years!"

She flips another cake, then turns to give me a snuggle. "Actually, the Victor Talking Machine Company, later RCA Victor, is even older than that. Mr. Eldridge Johnson started the business in 1901. Our apartment building, Building #17, was partially built in 1909, but the rest of it, including the Nipper tower, was completed in 1916. We're also celebrating the centennial of Building #2 across the street, which used to be the executive office building, with an auditorium on the 8th floor. It's now the Camden City School District Central Office. And one more: The Walt Whitman Art Center, cater-corner from us, with its reflecting pools and statues out front, is also a century old. It was presented as a library to the people of Camden by Eldridge Johnson, but now it's part of Rutgers University."

"Peter Pan is my favorite statue!" I interject.

"You and your Buckadee too," she laughs, as she hands me a glass of fresh-squeezed orange juice. *Yum.* "These three buildings, plus the deserted Building #8 on the other corner of Front and Cooper, where radios were built, are all that are left of the original thirty-eight Victor buildings." Deep breath.

"What was built in this building?" I ask.

"Cabinets for record players, which were called Victrolas. Plus, they built wings for airplanes here during World War I."

"Wow, GB, that's a lot of history to absorb before breakfast!" GB is my nickname for Grandma Butch.

"You're right, Jenna," she concedes. "But this is exciting stuff—Camden was the center of the recording industry. Right smack here. A whole century ago!"

Suddenly I'm aware that the soundtrack of our morning is the soft, gentle sound of harp music floating dreamily from behind the studio door.

"*Caro mio ben, credimi almen,*" Buckadee croons quietly. I can hardly hear her.

"Good morning, Buckadee! You can sing louder now. I'm up! And who is Geraldine Farrar?" I ask as I open the door to the library, which is also the office and the art and music studio. I love to look at Buckadee's harps, her illustrations, and all the books, plants, and tchotchkes. The giant old-fashioned clock over the bookcase tells me it's 8:50...*darn it all,* it's still raining....

—

10

Buckadee's sitting behind Edna the harp, looking like a bedraggled angel in her sweats and spectacles. She also looks a lot like her daughter Anna, my mom. Come to think of it, so do I. Except I'm a lot darker, and my hair's curly, as in afro. My mom's mixed, but looks white, and my dad's mixed too, but looks black. I'm somewhere in the middle, but look more black than white, so that's how I'm perceived. I'm considered black, and my mom and Buckadee are considered white, until people take the time to get to know us. Then they know that we're all mixed, and that, more importantly, we're family, and that we're people with opinions.

Buckadee comes out from behind Edna and gives me a giant bear hug. "I'm so happy that you're here, my Sweetie Pie! It works out perfectly that your parents decided to visit their friends in Manhattan this weekend, and to drop you off with us on the way. How was your drive up from D.C. last night? You were too tired to talk, so we tucked you in as soon as your daddy carried you through the door."

"I don't even remember getting here," I say. "I guess I fell asleep in the car. The trip took forever, 'cause of all the rain. It seemed as if Camden was like Emerald City in the Wizard of Oz. It just kept getting farther and farther away, and I just kept getting sleepier!"

"Well, by now you must be starving, so let's go get some of those pancakes," says Buckadee as she takes me by the hand. "We'll discuss Ms. Farrar over breakfast."

"Everything's ready except the fruit!" announces Grandma Butch.

"Let me help," I say as I stick a slotted spoon into the bowl of strawberries, raspberries, and blueberries, and start to scatter them over the steaming pancakes.

"I'll slice these peaches," adds Buckadee. "What a glorious table, Suz!" she says to her partner, Grandma Butch. She's right. The silver, glittery placemats, yellow flowers, and flickering faux candles are fun and inviting on this dreary morning. And the pancakes taste as good as they look.

I'm so happy to be here in Camden with two of my favorite people on the planet!

"I see you put a new picture on the wall," I say as I reach for more sliced peaches.

Buckadee takes it down and hands it to me, saying, "Here, check it out!" then heads over to the coffee pot for a refill.

I study the photo of Walt Whitman, with his intense stare and bushy beard, then read aloud, *"Camden was originally an accident, but I will never be sorry I was left over in Camden. It has brought me blessed returns."*

"That quotation is true for Buckadee and me too," says Grandma Butch. We moved here because we couldn't afford such a nice apartment across the river in Philadelphia. But now that we're here, we see that Camden is an awesome city. We love it, and want to stay here."

"So," says Buckadee, slowly. "What do you know so far about the city of Camden?"

"Hmm…" I squirm. "I learned some things about your neighborhood just this morning from GB," I answered.

"Good! But what did you know before that?" she persists. Mom and Dad were really upset when my grandmas moved here last year. I measure my words carefully. "Mom and Dad had…qualms…when you decided to move here. They said it was dangerous."

"It is," responds Grandma Butch, "but it's improving. There are plans. And hope. And lots of good caring people who live here, and who believe in Camden's future. Plus, like Uncle Christopher, there are so many artists, writers, and musicians right here in our neighborhood. Just like us! It's fabulous!"

"But, do you remember last summer, soon after you moved here, when we went to the art show in Haddonfield?" I ask. "We drove both ways on the street that runs from one town to the other."

"Yes, Haddon Avenue," answers Buckadee.

"Well, I noticed that Haddonfield had clean wide streets, lots of stores and restaurants and beautiful houses. Then we drove through Collingswood, which was really nice too, but not quite so ritzy. Then we stopped at the graveyard where we visited the poet Walt Whitman's little house."

"That's called a mausoleum," says Buckadee. "He's buried right inside."

"Oh yeah. And that's where I heard his voice coming out from behind the iron gate…." I shiver, but I'm not cold. "As soon as we started to drive back here, the road got bumpier, the houses and stores got smaller, and lots of them were boarded up and falling apart. And I saw trash lying around everywhere. And…the people I saw looked sadder—and darker."

"As always, you are very astute," observes Buckadee. "And correct. We live in a country where good jobs and good schools and housing are still denied to poor people—who are very often people of color, and to women of all colors, who are still underpaid compared to men." She sounds upset. "It's a catch-22. In other words, it's very difficult to get a good education, a fine job, and a house in, say, Haddonfield, if you're born poor with black skin in, say, Camden. It really doesn't make any sense why the schools and businesses and infrastructure in Haddonfield get lots of improvements, and the streets are kept clean and in good repair, but not so in the poorest sections of Camden. Ideally, as a country—and as a world—we should provide opportunities for a good life for *all* of our citizens. I mean, for goodness' sake, why not?"

"Just follow the money," comments Grandma Butch, always the realist. "The rich get richer and the poor get poorer because the system is set up that way."

"Well, let's change it!" I decree.

"That's the spirit!" yells GB. "Yes, let's!"

Suddenly we hear a tap on the door, and a dapper, white-haired gentleman appears, with his usual chipper smile.

"Uncle Christopher!" I exclaim.

—

14

3. Gerry and Satchmo

"What a joy to see you, Princess Jenna!" beams Uncle Christopher, as he bows deeply and kisses my hand. He's such a gentleman. He's not really my uncle, but I think of him as family. "I was hoping you'd be here. I was also hoping to greet a certain Ms. Geraldine Farrar, but I don't see her anywhere...."

"Oh, hold your horses, Christopher. She won't be making her appearance for several hours yet," says Buckadee with a toss of her head. "In the meantime, a certain granddaughter hasn't yet learned the history of our remarkable city."

"And I don't see any sign of Mr. Eldridge Johnson, either, I might add," says GB with a wink to me.

"Touché!" says Uncle Christopher, looking wounded. "I'll admit, he hasn't yet donned his bowler hat and spats. But he'll be appropriately decked out for this afternoon's festivities, and ready to read his memoirs to the adoring crowd."

"Eldridge Johnson started the Victor Talking Machine Company in 1901!" I announce proudly.

"Well, I'd say our Jenna does, indeed, know some local history!" smiles Uncle Christopher.

"Somebody please tell me about Geraldine Farrar!" I plead. "I've been hearing her name all morning!"

"Yes, it's about time," admits Buckadee. "Ms. Farrar was a very popular singer back in the early days of recorded music. She was also an actress in the silent movies, and a very dramatic personality. Lots of young women fans would gather around her. They were called 'Gerry-flappers' back in the 1920s."

"Was she as popular as Queen Bey?" I ask.

"Yes! But she sang mostly opera—which was considered the height of coolness back in the day."

"So, she was seriously stylin'," I declare.

"Indeed, and she was recorded right here in Camden!" adds Uncle Christopher. "Plus she performed for the big-wigs of the Victor Talking Machine Company and their guests on the huge stage that still exists up on the eighth floor of Building #2, right across the street. Come over here and look out the window," he beckons. I observe a dingy-looking big old building, eight stories tall. It's still raining. "Your Buckadee and I had a tour up there with Mr. Fred Barnum, who wrote a book about the company. The stage is still there, but, in order to see the top part of it, you have to climb up to a balcony and peer out over a ceiling that was added later. Now the whole area is used for storage, and no one seems to be aware of the grandeur that was once there. It was the first auditorium in the world where a whole orchestra was recorded! The Boston and then the Philadelphia Orchestras were each recorded there back in 1917. After that, sound recording was done in Building #15, which was built—right outside there, where you see the parking lot. So the big stage in Building #2 was then used to showcase the performers who recorded with the Victor Talking Machine Company, besides Geraldine Farrar, like...let's see...Enrico Caruso, Louis Armstrong...."

"His nickname was Satchmo!" I chime in. "He recorded What a Wonderful World, and our chorus sang it for the spring concert."

"Beautifully, I might add," beams Buckadee.

"Yes indeed! And then there was Jascha Heifetz, the violinist.... I used to listen to his albums all the time when I was a kid. What a talent!" GB says with a wistful smile.

Buckadee continues, "And there were other popular opera singers, like Madame Emma Calve, Nellie Melba, and Alma Gluck, and, yes, Caruso, who used to sing duets with Geraldine Farrar."

"Camden was where the recording industry was born. Heavens, such an exciting time it must have been!" adds Uncle Christopher. Then, "I know, let's go over to my apartment and sing some songs! Mary, I mean Buckadee, you can rest your fingers, since you'll be playing the harp later, and I'll play my piano. Whattaya say?" Hey, it sounds good to me. I love Uncle Christopher's apartment, with its red curtains, antique toys, and his paintings and piano. Plus, he has even more windows in his living room, with the same view of Building #2 and the Ben Franklin Bridge. You can see the Delaware River flowing underneath the bridge, and, sometimes, giant barges with their tugboats. I hope this rain stops and we can all take a walk on the "esplanade" along the river. Oh, that's right, we have the Nipper Fest. Well, maybe tomorrow we'll have time for a stroll,

---

plus a visit to the Aquarium and Children's Garden—or a ferry ride to the Spruce Street Park in Philly! Gosh, I'd love to live here in the Nipper Building....

"So Jenna," inquires Uncle Christopher in a cheerful voice, after we walk the few steps to his apartment, "what should we sing?" He seats himself at the grand piano.

"Do you know any Beyoncé or Alabama Shakes?" I ask. He shakes his head. "Or Justin Bieber or Taylor Swift?" His smile is turning upside down.

Buckadee cuts in, "Jenna asks me the same questions, Christopher, and I just don't perform any of their songs yet, although I love Alabama Shakes. That Brittany Howard is awesome!"

"Hmm, how about Rude?" Uncle Christopher asks hopefully.

"Yay! I love it!" And I jump up and down to prove it.

We all join in, and sing, laugh, talk, and laugh some more. Then I ask Uncle Christopher to perform his famous Nipper's Yap Rap, a funny song he wrote about the little fox terrier whose image became the Victor company trademark. In the picture, Nipper looks quizzically at an old-fashioned Victrola. The painting, done over a hundred years ago, is called His Master's Voice. I guess the little fellow was confused as to how his big master could have climbed inside that little machine and then started talking, or maybe singing. In real life, that nasty little doggie loved to nip people on their ankles. Hence his name.

"Lunch time!" announces Grandma Butch, rubbing her growling belly.

"Can we go downstairs to the Victor's Pub?" I ask hopefully.

"Sure!" answers Buckadee. "Can you join us, Christopher?"

"I'm afraid I've got to begin my transition into being Mr. Eldridge Johnson," he says with a sly smile, "so I'll just munch a little lunch up here. I'll catch you all later—that is, if you even recognize me in my get-up!" he winks.

4. Glinda

"Let's take the freight elevator, it's closer!" I suggest, as I skip down the hallway.

"Sure," says GB, walking slowly with the help of her silver-studded cane. "By the way, Jenna…Buckadee and Christopher will be donning their costumes this afternoon for the Nipper Fest, and I'll be sitting with my painting at the art exhibit out in the courtyard—or in the lobby, if it's still raining. How would you like to be my assistant? You could answer any questions and show people around our makeshift gallery. Whattaya say?"

I stop so my grandmas can catch up to me. "Hmm, I don't know." I mean, how many questions would I even know the answers to? I hope I'm not hurting her feelings. "I mean, I'd rather just wander around and see what's going on, if that's OK with you. I wouldn't know what to say, GB! I'll just check in with you every so often." Uh-oh. She looks upset. "Or, hmm, how about I think about it over lunch? Maybe I'll feel braver on a full stomach."

"Ok, Sunshine. We'll talk about it over dessert."

Ding! Here's the elevator. "Hey, may I run down the stairs and meet you two at the bottom?" I ask. "I bet I can beat you!"

"It's five stories! Why don't you just stay with us?" answers Buckadee with a doubtful frown. She's holding on to GB's arm, 'cause GB's a little unsteady on her feet. Actually, I think Buckadee is too, but don't tell her I said so.

"Aw, I'll be fine. I promise I'll walk slowly and carefully. But wait for me downstairs!" I say as I push open the heavy door to the stairwell.

There's a rush of quiet after the door clunks shut behind me. I look around at the white plaster, brick, and concrete walls, as I walk down a hallway to another huge door, which leads to a little covered balcony outside. I take a deep breath of damp fresh air. Then I heave open yet another giant door that leads back inside to the staircase. *Cheesh!* I dutifully hold the banister as I carefully walk down to the fourth floor. There's a sign: "**STAIR #1, 4, YOU ARE 3 FLOORS ABOVE STREET.**" Ok, that's confusing. Three flights to go, I think. I can judge the stairs better now, and it's pretty bright in here, so I walk down a little faster. One more floor to go...two more floors to go...three more floors to go...four more floors to go...five more floors to go. I stop for air. Now wait a minute! I only had one more floor to go about three or four floors ago! Wow. I must be several stories below ground level! Gosh all fishhooks, this old factory is HUGE!

I turn around to climb back upstairs, but the stairs have all disappeared! I'm surrounded by four walls. Uh-oh. There's grayness all around me, not white anymore. Or has the light faded? No exit anywhere. I try not to panic, as I spin in circles, searching up, down, and sideways for an escape. I lean back against the wall to catch my breath. My heart is pounding. My grandmas are going to be beside themselves! They're probably looking around for me already.

Suddenly I feel my back shift position. The wall's moving! No, that's simply got to be my imagination...maybe I'm dizzy from spinning. There it goes again! I whisk around and see the wall glow and shimmer, then slowly disappear. I look up to see a stone arch where the concrete wall used to be, and a dimly-lit hallway. I start walking. After all, what other choice do I have?

Yipes, what's that! I jump as I feel something warm and purring rub against my leg. I look down into the near-darkness and see nothing. I blink and look again. Lo and behold—an adorable little black cat is looking up at me and softly meowing! I lean over and let her sniff my fingers, so she knows I'm friendly, then I gently pet her head, and she rubs her whole back and tail against my hand, purring even louder. Such soft fur! Like velvet, only softer. In fact, it's so soft that it's like water, or like the texture of absolutely nothing at all, if that's even possible. And it feels so good, like...happiness...like seeing my grandmothers again after being apart for two months. Oops—I stand up quickly. I've got to find my way back! My new little friend meows again and starts to trot down the hall toward a staircase. At least it goes up! I look behind me, and see that the stone archway has disappeared, leaving only a gray wall.

"Hey little kitty, wait for me!" I holler as I run after her. She's already disappeared around a curve in the staircase.

Whew! There she is, right in front of me again, gliding up more stairs to another hallway.

My eyes have adjusted to the semi-darkness, but it's still kind of hard to see. Is that a door up ahead? Yes! And...it's ajar. The little cat disappears inside. I stop cold. Soft music is playing in there, and I hear a woman's gentle voice....

"Glinda, you're back, you sweet thing! Did you bring her with you like I asked? *Jenna!* Are you there? Please come in, I've been waiting for you forever!"

5. Aunt Cora

I'm frozen to the floor. I can't move. Then, slowly, gradually, by its own accord, my hand reaches out and gently touches the door. It swings open by itself, and I'm suddenly bathed in a soft golden light, with the scent of chocolate wafting through the air, and the rapturous strains of a violin singing faintly, but delectably, in my ears. The music seems to be coming from a large rectangular wooden box in the far corner of this cozy little room. Suddenly I see her. No, first of all I feel her warm smile. The woman rises from her rocking chair, reaching out her hand for mine.

"Hello, Jenna. I'm your Great-Great-Great Aunt Cora, but you can just call me Aunt Cora. That would be a lot easier, and save time, wouldn't you say?"

It isn't the wart that draws my eyes to her face—although the wart is truly spectacular. I just can't look away, even though I'm being rude. It's this: the love. I've never ever seen such a loving face. Aunt Cora simply makes my heart melt with happiness. I take her hand, and it's as soft and warm as little Glinda's fur.

I open my mouth to speak, but no sound comes out.

"Oh, my dear, you must be…incredulous," she admits in her lovely voice. "I can't even imagine what a surprise all this must be for you. You thought you were heading downstairs to meet your grandmothers, and here you are with me! Ha-ha!" Her laughter sounds like a bubbling brook trickling through an enchanted forest.

"Life can really blindside us with its little twists and turns, *n'est pas?*" she says with a smile as she leads me gently to a small green velvet sofa, which has flowing wooden carvings above the back cushion, and beneath our feet lies a Persian carpet with intricate red and blue designs, and gold accents. Crimson velvet drapes cover most of the wall space, and a large potted palm sits by the rectangular box, which has a handle protruding from one side, and which I now realize is an old-fashioned record player. No doubt a Victrola. All the furnishings look, I'd say, Victorian. On the back of her upholstered blue velvet rocking chair is a crocheted doily. What does Buckadee call those things? Oh yes, that would be an antimacassar.

"Here, Jenna, I've made you some cocoa with a little whipped cream on top. It's not too hot to drink," she says, as she places the delicate cup and saucer, white with pink roses and a gold rim, on a small oval coffee table in front of me. I'm shaking a little too hard to even think of picking it up yet, but it smells divine.

"My Buckadee told me that her grandmother had a sister named Cora who died during the Spanish flu epidemic in 1918." My voice is faint, but at least it's there.

Aunt Cora sits back down in her rocking chair, and I see a shadow of sadness cross her face. "Yes, that would be me. My three little daughters and my husband and I all passed away within a short time, back in October of 1918. It was right before my thirty-first birthday. My mother died at age thirty as well, from typhoid fever, back in 1887. So tragic. But, thankfully, life goes on. Not in the same way, for sure, but...how can I say this? The journey continues. Yes, it does. And, for the past nine years, I've been keeping an eye on you, Jenna, hoping to meet you in person."

"But why me?" I ask. "You've got plenty of relatives by now...all my cousins and their parents and grandparents. Probably hundreds of them!"

"Oh, I've kept an eye on them all, but I've always felt a special affinity for you. I guess you remind me of myself when I was your age. And I like the way your mind works. You're destined to be a loving person and a creative thinker—actually, you already are—and that's very special indeed." I look deeply into her intense blue eyes, and note that her hair is black and tightly curled, just like mine, although her skin looks much lighter than mine. Her face is lovely, although some fuddy-duddies might think the wart on her nose isn't overly attractive. Aunt Cora, however, wears that wart with aplomb; in fact, she celebrates it! Just by being on her face, the wart becomes as beautiful as she is. I'd say she still looks to be around thirty, although...hmmm...that's pretty remarkable, since she died, let me think, ninety-eight years ago....

So many questions are running through my befuddled brain, but I blurt out, "I'm happy to meet you, Aunt Cora, and your cat too, but my grandmothers are probably very worried about me right now." I stand up to leave.

24

"No, they're not," she says with a little smile. "One benefit of living on the other side of life is that I can work with time. Let me explain. Well, actually, it's quite hard to explain, but I can tell you that whenever you decide to go back to the elevator to meet them, you'll be the first to arrive. They won't miss you for a second. You see, since I've crossed over..."

"You mean, since you died?" I ask. I know I'm being too blunt, but I'd really like to clear up my overwhelming confusion.

"Yes, you could say that I died, but I really don't like to use that word, since, obviously, I'm not really dead, now am I?" she asks with a twinkle in her eye.

"No, I guess not," I say as I sit back down. Glinda rubs against my legs.

"So, since I've crossed over, there are things I can do simply by wanting to. You have this power too, except for maybe the time-bending part, and I'd like to help you discover yourself a bit more than you have already, if you'll allow me. Actually, that's why I've summoned you here. I hope you're not angry with me."

"No, no. Not angry at all," I say as I reach for my cocoa. It should be quite cold by now, but it's not. *OMG—this stuff's to DIE for!* No, Jenna, don't you *dare* say that out loud, I think to myself as the chocolate flavor bursts on my tongue like a thousand happy hugs.

All I say is, *"Yum!"*

6. Gesundheit!

"So, Jenna, ask me some questions!" commands Aunt Cora with a smile.

"Hmm, I hear harp music coming from the Victrola now," I observe. "Is that Buckadee playing?"

"It is," says Aunt Cora. "I've always loved her gentle touch on the strings. So soothing, so ethereal. I tried to meet your Buckadee once, when she was nine years old, just like you are."

"What happened?"

"Well, she seemed to realize that someone was there, but she looked around and saw nothing. Jenna, you're the only one in the whole wide world who has ever seen me or heard me. I had a feeling you were special—and I was right!"

"Did you lure her down into a magical basement like you did me?"

"Isn't this place fantastic?" she beams. "No, I sat on a branch next to her way up high in a pine tree. Could that kid ever climb!"

I laugh, picturing Buckadee with scraped knees, long unkempt braids, and sticky, pungent pine sap on her hands. "So, are you always here? Is this your home now?" I ask.

"I have many homes. I live fully inside each moment, and each moment is an eternity. I spend time with my three daughters, but now I'm spending time with you, my Jenna. So, for this moment, this is my home. Right here in Camden with you." She looks at me with love in her eyes. "Speaking of which, I understand you've been learning about Camden just this morning over breakfast," says Aunt Cora, studying my face. "There's quite a history here, isn't there?"

"Yeah," I comment, "but some of this city is a hot mess."

"Please don't speak harshly of Camden," she admonishes. "You see, this is a magical city, with lots of heart and a bright future. We must believe in Camden in order for her to thrive, and it's really important for those of us who love this city to understand her whole story. Hmm, I have a fun idea..." She stops to think for a second or two. "Let's visit Camden in say, 1926," she suggests, smiling, and reaching for her awesome wart. "Did you ever hear of the Sesquicentennial?"

"Not really," I answer, wondering what other surprises could possibly be in store for me. "Doesn't that mean a hundred and fifty years?"

"Correct," she beams. "And Philadelphia was chosen as the national site for the United States' Sesquicentennial Celebration of 1926, when we celebrated the one hundred and fiftieth anniversary of the signing of the Declaration of Independence, which, of course, had taken place in Philadelphia."

"On July 4, 1776!" I pipe in. "Although, actually...Congress approved it that day, but it wasn't officially signed until August 2."

"Correct again!" smiles Aunt Cora. "And Camden, being a very important city, was part of the Sesqui celebration as well. In fact, the festivities included the grand opening of the brand new Delaware River Bridge running between Camden and Philly, which you now call the Ben Franklin. Before that, the only public transportation between the two cities was the ferry boat, in fact, several—which, back then, were large enough to accommodate the passengers as well as their cars and horses! So the bridge, which was finished just in time for the Fourth of July, was a big deal, indeed. The whole Sesqui was a huge affair—actually a world's fair, including international exhibitors, and lasted from May through November. Even the President of the United States came to both cities to celebrate! Do you know who he was?"

I put on my thinking cap... "Calvin Coolidge?"

"You're amazing!" she smiles, then gives her wart another little tap.

Now Aunt Cora stands up and smooths her long blue skirt, which quickly shortens, as I watch, to mid-calf length. Her skirt has turned to beige, trimmed with ivory lace and dusty-rose ribbons. Dusty-rose is one of my favorite colors. I look down in time to see my blue jeans morph into a smaller version of Aunt Cora's outfit. I'm not so sure I want to wear a skirt, but, for now, I'm not gonna rock the boat. This boat's already rockin'!

"Come here, Jenna. Let's see how we look," she says, smiling gleefully, as she grasps my hand and leads me over to a large oval mirror framed by dark carved wood, standing in the corner. She smooths back her hair, which is in long black braids wrapped around her head, and, *presto!* Her hairstyle becomes short and bobbed, right out of the roaring twenties! Aunt Cora now reminds me of Esther Jones, the beautiful African American entertainer from the twenties known as Baby Esther, with the baby voice, who inspired the Betty Boop cartoons. She reaches over and smooths my hair as well. I look closely in the mirror as my longish, rather unkempt afro shortens into a neat curly bob, just like Aunt Cora's. We look like a very stylin' mother and daughter duo—from 1926.

"Boop oop a doop!" I sing with a giggle.

"Onward!" commands my quirky aunt, and we prance out the door, leaving Glinda to play with an extra piece of dusty-rose ribbon that has fallen to the floor.

As we climb the concrete stairs, I grasp Aunt Cora's hand until my brown knuckles turn white. Suddenly we burst outside, and I sneeze from the brightness. It isn't pouring anymore, but it isn't sunny either. I sneeze again as I look up and see giant chimneys spewing thick smoke.

"Where ARE we?" I ask, confused. I feel my skirt blow against my legs, as a mini-whirlwind of ashes and dust plays across our path.

"Right here by the Victor—just ninety years ago, that's all," answers my stylin' escort. I look around and see that we came out of the Front Street exit, but there are so many more buildings than I remember! And covered passageways running between them, way up high.

"That must be Building #15, where the recording studios are," I observe. "Right there where we normally park our car!" We walk over to the corner of Cooper Street. "And it looks like there's another factory right next to it, filling up the rest of the parking lot."

"That's the Esterbrook Steel Pen Manufacturing Company," explains Aunt Cora, as she takes my hand, "which was one of the first pen factories in the whole country. The very first, the C. Howard Hunt Pen Company, is also in Camden." She looks both ways, and we wait for a horse and buggy and a classic Model T Ford to go by. Then across the street we go, right toward Building #2— appearing a lot newer and brighter than it did earlier this morning. "I hope we're not late for our appointment!"

"Appointment?" I ask, as I notice a gaggle of giggly young women milling around outside the front entrance, chatting excitedly. "Whoa! I wonder what's going on?"

"Well, I understand that Geraldine Farrar is presenting a recital up in the eighth floor auditorium this afternoon," comments my mysterious auntie.

"Gerry-flappers!"

"Indeed!" she laughs, as we sweep past them and through the door.

"Mrs. Cora Kahler and her niece, Miss Jenna Long?" asks the guard. She nods, and he bows deeply and announces, "Mr. Johnson is expecting you."

"Mr. *Eldridge* Johnson?" I blurt out.

"Yes, Miss—but of course!" he replies. "Mr. Johnson is the owner of The Victor Talking Machine Company. Please follow me." He leads us brusquely through a fancy white entrance hall, with a high ceiling framed by ornate moldings and a huge glass and gold filigree chandelier. There are several Greek pillars, and I see an elegant arch curving over the marble staircase, which we pass on our way to the elevator.

"Please," our escort directs the elevator operator, a rather portly African American gentleman, who, like the guard, sports a crisp, neat, navy blue uniform, "these ladies are special guests of Mr. Johnson. He's expecting them in his office." Then he bows again, as he turns on his heel and returns to his post by the front door.

The elevator operator pushes the button for Floor #7, then stands at attention as we ascend. I must look scared, because he suddenly smiles and winks at me, then goes back to looking serious.

We step out onto an elegant, wide white hallway, with large mahogany desks by each door...at least eight or ten, I'd say. At each desk sits a very prim lady, looking neat and businesslike. One of them stands and crosses over to us, her hand extended.

"Welcome, Mrs. Kahler and Miss Long! Mr. Johnson has been anticipating your visit." She gently but firmly shakes our hands, then beckons, "Please follow me." She leads us though an entranceway into a cavernous reception room, which has a fireplace, and impressive, deep rich dark brown carved wood everywhere I look. It's such a contrast to the white hallway. She walks across the room and knocks lightly on another beautifully carved door.

"Are they here?" comes from the next room, as the door swings open and a very dapper looking gentleman sweeps across the room to greet us.

"Cora!" he says, smiling, as he bows deeply and kisses her hand—just like Uncle Christopher does! "It's been too long. What a pleasure to see you again! And this must be your niece, Jenna. How do you do, young lady? I've heard so much about you!" I get a bow and a kissed hand, too. "Please, please, come into my office and take a seat. Let's catch up!" He leads us into the next room, his inner sanctum, which is also quite impressive, with its own fireplace, dark carved wood, and deep, plush, large leather chairs. We all sit around a massive mahogany desk, as another woman enters the room and sets down a tray with a teapot, cups, sugar, cream, spoons, napkins, and sugar cookies; also some slices of lemon, in case one prefers lemon to cream. Mr. Johnson stands up to graciously serve us himself.

32

"My dear Eldridge," says Aunt Cora, with a twinkle in her eye, "it's startling to see what you've achieved over the past twenty-five years. Explain yourself!"

"Yes, I'll admit, I've surprised even *me*. It seems like yesterday when I was finally able to own my own machine shop, right across the street here in Camden, but it was a struggle; I was hardly getting by. Then one day a fellow walked in and asked me to improve upon a contraption invented by a Mr. Emile Berliner. Now wait a moment," Mr. Johnson pauses. "Let me go back a few more years and explain."

"Yes, please do!" I add. "This is getting seriously interesting!"

"Well, you see," begins my new acquaintance, smiling at me, "recorded sound officially started in 1857, with an invention, dubbed the phonautograph, by a French scientist named Leon Scott de Martinville. He was able to trace sound waves onto a cylinder. In 1877, Thomas Alva Edison made a similar discovery, and was able to record the human voice. He was issued a United States patent the next year for a 'Phonograph or Speaking Machine.' But Edison also used cylinders. Emile Berliner came up with the idea of a flat disk, instead of a cylinder, and the disk made it possible to create a master record, from which duplicate copies could be made."

"So you could make lots of copies, and then start a business," I say.

"Yes, but the Berliner Gramophone had to be run by hand, so it couldn't maintain a constant pitch," says Mr. Johnson. "That's where I came in. I was asked to figure out how to add a spring motor, so that it could play properly. I worked on it, but they didn't like my original design—but then, I didn't like their original machine! It was badly designed. It sounded like a partially educated parrot with a sore throat and a cold in the head, but the little wheezy instrument caught my attention and held it fast and hard. I became interested in it as I had never been interested in anything before."

"And the rest is history!" sings out Aunt Cora.

"Yes, indeed," agrees Eldridge Johnson. "I followed my dream, never gave up, and now we have The Victor Talking Machine Company, which produces thousands of Victrolas, radios, Radiolas, records, and, more recently, we're even working on new-fangled motion picture soundtracks! I'm a multi-millionaire—whoever would have guessed?" He looks wistful. "And now I'm thinking about selling…retiring."

"You're kidding!" Aunt Cora's eyes open wide.

"No, Cora, I'm not kidding. My business is more than established, and I have more than enough money. Now I'd like to take the time to enjoy it—and to do something useful with it." He smiles.

"But you have already, Eldridge!" says my aunt.

"I try," he concedes. "Jenna, come over here to the window and see the library and garden I've created." I wipe cookie crumbs off my mouth, then hurry over to the window. There I see Johnson Park, with its statues, especially my favorite. Lots of kids are cavorting around the park, laughing and playing in the wading pool. Some grown-ups are sitting on park benches, talking, eating lunch, watching the little ones. One daring lady is even holding her skirt up to her knees and cooling her bare feet in the water.

"I love the statue of Peter Pan," I announce.

"We'll be celebrating the installation of that statue this September," he adds. "In fact, we'll be holding a pageant on September 24, when local schoolchildren, over 3,000 of them, will be depicting scenes from J. M. Barrie's fabulous story. You'll have to come and join us!"

He pulls out his gold pocket watch, his eyes open wide, and he exclaims, "Oh my goodness gracious! We'd better head on upstairs to the auditorium! It's almost time for Ms. Farrar to begin her recital!"

34

"Where is everybody?" I ask as we exit the elevator into the grand auditorium. "I thought Geraldine Farrar was giving a recital this afternoon!"

"Oh, she is, indeed," responds Mr. Johnson, taking my arm like gentlemen used to do in the olden days, or so I've read, "but she'll be presenting a private concert exclusively for you and your Aunt Cora."

"But what about all the Gerry-flappers outside?" I ask, alarmed.

"*Gerry-flappers?*" I hear from across the large hall. I look, but can't see anyone. Suddenly the spotlight goes on, and there she is in all her glory, standing regally at center stage. Aunt Cora and I gasp as one. Geraldine Farrar looks like a queen, her auburn hair bedecked in pearls and beads and flowers, wearing an elegant long gown, her bejeweled shoes peeking out from underneath.

"Is that my *Cora?*" she asks, smiling broadly, "and is this her magnificent niece, Jenna?" She swoops off the stage and down the aisle to hug us both. She smells like gardenias. Then she looks serious. "Jenna, did you say Gerry-flappers are milling about outside?" I nod. "Ah, I used to have such a fan club when I was still singing opera in New York, but I didn't realize that those lovely young women were still following me, after all this time. How unutterably divine!" she says with a flourish. Then her brow furrows; she's obviously deep in thought. "After spending the morning recording across the street in the studio, I was escorted over here by way of the underground tunnel…then we took the private freight elevator up here to my dressing room, where I took some refreshment, rested, and changed into my costume. I never looked out the front windows at all, so I simply had no idea. How wonderful that they're here! Please, Eldridge, let them come up for the recital! I *insist!*"

"Me too!" I chime in.

"Well, in that case," acquiesces Mr. Johnson, "it will be done." He nods to his assistant, who hurriedly heads back to the elevator, her heels clicking on the hardwood floor.

I look across the room and see a table heavily laden with good things to eat: a variety of tea sandwiches of all possible shapes and fillings—even peanut butter and jelly—a crystal punchbowl full of lemonade, with paper-thin slices of lemon and sprigs of spearmint floating on top, and another cut-glass bowl full of fresh fruit salad—what giant juicy red strawberries, and big chunks of fresh pineapple—surrounded by garlands of red and green grapes. And what a centerpiece! In the middle of the table towers a 6-tiered cream-colored cake on a pedestal, decorated with real dusty-rose colored roses, which cascade down to the lacey beige tablecloth. I reach over and squeeze Aunt Cora's hand.

"Oh, Cora, it's so good to see you again," gushes Ms. Farrar.

"Gerry, you look downright exquisite. I've read the reviews in the paper, and they're saying that you're a 'charismatic innovator.' I completely agree. You know, my dear Geraldine, beyond all that, you are the most magical performer I've ever observed on a stage," declares Aunt Cora with her beautiful smile.

"Magical? You, my dear, have the corner on THAT!" laughs Gerry. "Oh my goodness gracious...I can't wait to catch up! However, for now, you two will simply have to excuse me. I have some scrumptious surprises in store for you this afternoon, so I'd better scurry on backstage and prepare!" And off she sweeps toward the stage, gliding like Glinda.

We choose seats in the front row, as the lights blink on and off.

"That means the show will begin in a few minutes!" says Aunt Cora in a low voice. There's a hush. At that moment, we hear the ecstatic voices of at least twenty giggling, whispering Gerry-flappers rustling their stylish selves into their seats right behind us. I turn around to watch in wonder, as the lights begin to dim, then they go out altogether, and I turn back just in time to see the curtain slowly begin to rise. I can hardly stand it, I'm so excited!

Which means, come to think of it, that I'm a Gerry-flapper too!

9. A Magical Performance

Awesome. Geraldine Farrar stands before us in all her splendor. After a moment's hush, we burst into applause. As the clapping starts to diminish, our queen takes a step forward.

"Welcome everyone! What an absolute pleasure it is for me to be here with you today! I'm especially honored to have two very special guests with us—my lovely young Miss Jenna Long, and her enchanting aunt, Mrs. Cora Kahler, a dear friend whom I seldom get to see, but whom I utterly adore." She gazes at her friend with a lingering smile. "My first song is a tribute to you, Cora. It's an art song from three centuries ago, but it remains as timely as ever. The poet is unknown, but the composer was Edward Purcell. At the piano is a true virtuoso, who has graciously agreed to accompany me on this special day: Mr. Sergei Rachmaninoff!" More applause erupts, as Mr. Rachmaninoff stands, bows, then sits back down with a flourish and begins to play, exquisitely. Geraldine sings:

"There is a lady, sweet and kind,
was never face so pleas'd my mind.
I did but see her passing by,
and yet I love her till I die.

Her gesture, motion and her smiles,
her wit, her voice, my heart beguiles.
Beguiles my heart, I know not why,
and yet I love her till I die.

Cupid is winged and doth range,
her country so my love doth change.
But change she earth or change she sky,
yet will I love her till I die."

Her voice is so very lovely and intriguing—even mesmerizing—and the combination of her expressive voice with the piano harmonies in the third verse...whew! I have the shivers!

Geraldine's next song was written by Mr. Rachmaninoff, himself. Even though he's Russian, she sings it in English, just for us.

"Night, on her muted lyre,
evokes with magic fingers the unforgotten sound
which in my heart still lingers."

I think she's thinking of Aunt Cora again…

"I feel your presence near me and I call your name
into the startled void.
I wait, I strain my sight.
Lo, nothing can I see, and nothing answers me.
Only your name floats on the
silent breath of night."

Breathtaking, indeed! After the applause starts to fade, we're treated to more surprises.

"Now I'd like to introduce two more Victor artists, Edna Phillips on the harp and Mr. Jascha Heifitz on violin!"

Buckadee told me that, in 1930, Edna Phillips was hired to be the principal harpist—and the first woman—in the Philadelphia Orchestra; and Sergei Rachmaninoff said that the Philadelphia Orchestra was "the finest orchestra the world has ever heard." And GB is such a fan of Mr. Heifitz. Wow, would my grandmas ever be in heaven right now! Another curtain rises behind the piano, and there they are, ready to perform, Edna's golden harp twinkling in the spotlight.

"I'd also like to present three of my favorite singers, who also record for the Victor Talking Machine Company: Nellie Melba, the most popular personage in Australia, Emma Calve, who has single-handedly turned Paris on its ear, and Alma Gluck, who is from Romania, but who is now a bright star right here in America! These are three of the most famous women in the whole wide world, so you might think that we're competitors, and we are," she winks and smiles, and everyone laughs. "On the other hand, we challenge and inspire each other to strive to do our very best work. I know that I'm a much more accomplished singer because of these remarkable and gifted artists. So, more than just competitors, we're actually colleagues, mentors, and friends." The applause is deafening as the three singers, glamourous in their long gowns and confident faces, make their grand entrance onto the stage to join Geraldine Farrar.

They all hold hands and, together, sing the same Italian song I heard Buckadee singing just this morning, *"Caro mio ben, credimi almen, sense di te, languisce il cor."* Seriously, my grandmothers would simply be freaking out right now! I can't wait to tell them!

Geraldine then cries out, "Oh, how I miss our dear friend, Enrico Caruso, who was such a magnificent tenor. He passed away almost five years ago, but I miss him more than ever today." Her voice catches, as she fights off her tears. Out of the corner of my eye I see my aunt reach for the magical bump on her nose.

"Ahhh!" Suddenly there's a gasp in the auditorium as the great Caruso himself appears. He strides across the stage to Geraldine and takes her in his arms. They both laugh, then cry, then, together, with the help of all the spectacular performers on the stage, they sing *O Soave Fanciulla* from the opera La Boheme.

I've honestly never experienced anything so rapturously beautiful in my whole life.

The applause is so deafening that I turn around. The auditorium is now packed full to the brim! Who are all these elegant women and men who are standing, applauding, crying, laughing, and hollering *Bravo!* They're all dressed to the nines, and sporting rapturous smiles. I see Mr. Johnson in the row right behind me, surrounded by ecstatic Gerry-flappers, and grinning broadly. He winks at me.

We're all standing up for the ovation, so I figure the recital must be over, and I start thinking about heading on over to that enticing refreshment table. That last number simply had to be the grand finale. It could never be topped. *Ever.*

But no.

Geraldine moves to the front of the stage and raises her hand. The ovation subsides, and she smiles, although her eyes are still glistening from her tears.

"My next guest is the very first person of color to record the Blues!" she announces. "She recorded her Crazy Blues in 1920, and this year, 1926, she recorded right here for Victor. She's a vaudeville singer, dancer, pianist and actress. She's been dubbed First Lady of the Blues and Queen of the Blues. She's also Queen of my heart, and the hearts of America. Please welcome the one and only…Mamie Smith!"

Miss Smith makes a dramatic entrance, wearing a glimmering black sequined gown and flaunting a large fan of white feathers, with more white feathers adorning her hair. She bows and smiles, then sits regally at a second grand piano, which has appeared on the stage facing Mr. Rachmaninoff's piano. She plays a bluesy riff, which gets instant applause.

"Two more introductions to go, then we'll begin our final selection," announces Geraldine. "Now, please join me in welcoming the one, the only…Louis Armstrong!"

"Satchmo!" I yell out loud, then clap my hand over my mouth. The famous singer and trumpeter struts onto the stage, playing the same blues riff that Mamie was playing. The audience goes wild!

"For our final number, I'd like to invite one more very special guest up on the stage." She pauses, then looks right at…*ME.*

"Everybody, please welcome *Miss Jenna Long!*" She reaches out her hand toward me, and I momentarily freeze. Aunt Cora gives me a squeeze, then a tiny little shove. I come to my senses and stand up on shaky legs. What in the world could I do up on that stage with all those famous people?? I smooth my lacey dress, then walk toward the stage, then up the steps, focusing totally on not falling down in a heap. So far so good. I walk right over to Ms. Farrar, who clasps my hand in hers.

"What would you like to sing, my dear?" she asks.

I think for a moment. "What a Wonderful World," I answer. She looks befuddled, and I think to myself, *Uh-oh! That song wasn't even recorded until the nineteen-sixties!* I glance, panicking, toward my aunt—just as she reaches for her miraculous wart.

Suddenly everyone nods, smiling in recognition, and the music begins. Satchmo plays a spectacular introduction on his trumpet, or is it his cornet? Then Mamie Smith and Edna Phillips and Heifitz and Rachmaninoff all join in. When it comes time to start singing, I actually don't feel afraid, and my voice rings out loud and clear! I sing the first part,

> *"I see leaves of green, red roses too,*
> *I see them bloom for me and you,*
> *and I think to myself,*
> *What a Wonderful World!"*

Then I reach out my arms and gesture to all on stage to join in. What a joy to hear those voices together with mine! Louis Armstrong, Geraldine Farrar, Mamie Smith, Nellie Melba, Enrico Caruso, Alma Gluck, and Madame Calve. *OMG, what a feeling!*

As soon as we're all done with the song, I step forward, stage center, and holler *"ENCORE!"* with my arms extended to the audience. Aunt Cora is beaming. I lock arms with Geraldine, and we all join the audience in singing the whole song again.

> *"The colors of the rainbow,*
> *so pretty in the sky,*
> *I see them on the faces*
> *of people passing by.*
> *I see friends shaking hands,*
> *saying How do you do?*
> *What they're really saying is*
> *I Love You…"*

When we sing the final *"What a Wonderful World,"* everyone stands and applauds. I mean EVERYONE: the whole audience and all of us on the stage. We're all beaming and looking at each other with joy and love. Black and white, old and young, female and male, famous and not yet famous.

I've never even imagined anything so divine!

The next thing I know, Aunt Cora and Eldridge Johnson are crossing over to the stage. Cora presents bright red roses to Gerry, and Eldridge presents—yup, you guessed it—beautiful dusty-rose-colored roses to little ole me.

11. Stylin' Wheels

Ok. So far, I haven't spilled a thing…well, except for one ornery blueberry that decided to roll right off my fancy little glass plate and land on the floor, and then I managed to step on it by mistake when I backed up to look for it. But at least it disappeared. I think it's still stuck to my shoe.

On the other hand, I've been meeting some amazing people— and I even signed some autographs! There are now officially a couple of Jenna-flappers in this room!

"Miss Jenna!" I turn around to see who's talking, and there's Mamie Smith! I grasp her hand in mine. "I'm oh, so proud to see a young woman of color standing tall on the stage," she says with emotion.

"What an honor to meet you, Miss Smith!" I say in awe.

"Well, it's a thrill for me to meet you, too," she replies. "I jes' hope you hold onto that positive attitude I saw in you today. It will take you far." She looks thoughtful. "It's an uphill battle for those of us with dark skin, you know. My music's popular now, and I'm grateful for that, but when I go on tour to perform my songs, I can't even stay at a hotel or eat in a restaurant because of my blackness. Bigotry. Prejudice. Racism. Hate. Makes no sense at all."

"It'll get better," I say, with not much conviction. Really, ninety years later, we still have a ways to go. I'm thinking of Sandra Bland, Trayvon Martin, Tamir Rice, and so many others. Plus I, for one, never even heard of Mamie Smith until today, and isn't that a shame. "It's hard for women, too," I add, thinking that I also had never heard of Geraldine Farrar, Nellie Melba, Madame Calve or Alma Gluck before today either, and they were actually just as famous as Enrico Caruso was during their lifetimes. I knew about Caruso, though—he even has the main lounge named after him in the Nipper Building, with his picture on the wall!

"Yeah, that's for sure. We women have it tough no matter what color we are. So being black and female's a double whammy, eh?" says Mamie Smith. We stand in silence, pondering.

"Cheer up, ladies!" says Satchmo, joining us. "What a jivin' time we jes' had up on that stage! Our show was the bee's knees! Gerry and Eldridge sure know how to host a shindig. Hold on to this memory forever, and it will help you on your journey. Whenever I start to feel in the dumps, I'll just think myself back to this day and smile." He gives Mamie an affectionate squeeze.

"Me too!" adds Geraldine, joining the three of us, holding Cora by the hand.

"Yes! We'll *schep naches!"* adds Alma Gluck.

"Indeed!" smiles Jascha Heifitz. "That's just what my mother always said."

"And Toots, too!" I say with a twinge of sadness. To *schep naches* is an old Yiddish expression that Grandma Butch's mother used to use. It means to take a wonderful moment, like this afternoon, when everyone is happy and creative and loving, and think about it with a smile when life turns around and hands you lemons.

"Oh my good heavens," says Geraldine. "What an amazing afternoon we're sharing. There for a moment, up on that stage, I even felt that Enrico was right there with us." A tear wells up and rolls down her cheek.

"Well, he *wa...*" I start to say.

"Yes, I felt the magic, too," cuts in Aunt Cora. "And now I'm afraid Jenna and I will be taking our leave. Her grandmothers will be expecting her."

"Oh no, not quite yet!" pleads Gerry. "You see, just yesterday I purchased a brand new Stutz Bearcat Roadster Convertible right over on Haddon Avenue—have you ever seen how very many car dealerships there are here in Camden?" She stops for a quick breath. "Anyway, I'd love to take you two for a spin over to see the new bridge! It just opened for the first time on July 1, which was, what? two days ago, and there'll be a big celebration there tomorrow for the Fourth, and President Coolidge will be officially dedicating it on the fifth, then planting a tree in Camden to commemorate it, but I must head to Manhattan today, so let's go take a look right now! What do you say, Cora? Can you spare a few more moments? Oh, please say yes!"

46

"The new Delaware River Bridge?" exclaims Aunt Cora. "Well, I'd say we'll just have to come along, Gerry! They've been building that bridge for close to five years now, and it's extraordinary!" Aunt Cora looks at me. "What do you say, Jenna? I think we can delay our departure a little longer."

"Great!" I say. I'm always up for an adventure, and I'd say this day continues to be the most awesome adventure *ever!!*

12. The Ben

"Whoopee!" laughs Gerry as she drives us up Cooper Street. All three of us have managed to squeeze together on the plush golden car seat. The exterior of the new 1926 Stutz is a deep, shiny, cherry red, and is this ever fun! Gerry steps harder on the gas, as her long emerald green and white polka-dotted chiffon scarf dances wildly behind her in the wind.

"Ooh, be careful!" I warn. "You don't wanna end up like Isadora Duncan!"

"Why ever not?" yells out Geraldine, looking puzzled, her long curls playfully cavorting around her lovely face. "She's one of my favorite dancers! Her free-form style of movement is so very cutting-edge; and I love her use of long, billowing scarves—just like this one! I visited her in Paris last year." She slows down to watch for oncoming traffic, then turns left onto Haddon Avenue.

Aunt Cora nudges me with her elbow, and I look over at her just as she surreptitiously touches her wart. All of a sudden I can hear her voice inside my head, even though her lips aren't moving.

Isadora Duncan didn't get strangled by her scarf while she was driving until 1927!

Oops, I think back to her, cringing. She winks.

"Look! Thar she blows!" announces Gerry. I'm sure that expression comes from sailors on whaling ships, but I use it all the time too. We had been able to see the bridge from the Victor complex, but, with all the extra buildings, and the smokestacks spewing their ashy fog, it wasn't a very satisfactory view. But NOW, what a sight! "You are now looking at the longest suspension bridge in the world—and we're about to drive on it!" she says with a *"Whoop!"* as we stop to pay the twenty-five cent toll.

We take it really slow. There's lots of traffic on the bridge, including other cars, horses with their riders, horses and buggies, and plenty of walkers on the sidewalk—all of us slowly savoring this delicious historic moment. After all, there had been talk about building this bridge for over a hundred years—and it's finally here!

I notice that, besides the road we're on, there are tracks for trains, a walkway for pedestrians, and tracks for trolleys, also called streetcars.

"Where are the trolleys and trains?" I ask.

"The trains aren't operating just yet, although there's already a bridge for trains a few miles further north." My aunt shakes her bobbed head, adding, "it looks like the streetcars will never start running at all. They even have trolley stations in the castle-like buildings on either end, and an underground station in Philly, but they aren't being used. By the time the bridge opened this week, trolleys were no longer popular. Now people are choosing to take a bus, or a horse, and more folks are owning their own cars. It looks like they're not even going to open the trolley tracks or stations at all...what a waste! I understand the inside of the streetcar stations in the towers have beautiful murals on the walls, depicting different forms of transportation, including ships, sailboats, steamboats, locomotives, stage coaches, even a dirigible."

"Speaking of transportation, check out that huge ship!" I say, as I look down to my left. "What a view!"

Gerry nods. "I heard that the New York Shipping Company, right here in Camden, is the largest shipping company IN THE WORLD!" she says with wonder. "It was originally to be built on Staten Island in New York, hence its name, but then the owners realized that Camden was a much better location, with more available land, transportation, and qualified laborers."

"Yes," nods Cora. "Jenna, that ship you see down there is the U.S.S. Saratoga, which was built here in Camden just last year. The largest ship ever built in North America!"

Then I spot some giant Campbell's soup cans, which are actually water towers, down below, over past the Nipper Building. Campbell's is still a huge company in 2016, and their world head-quarters is still in Camden; but, back in 1926, they also did all their manufacturing right here in town, where they made their condensed soup with New Jersey tomatoes.

Between Campbell's and the Victor Talking Machine Company and New York Ship, plus all the other businesses I see right here from the bridge, including Esterbrook Pens and a giant Van Sciver's furniture company, I begin to grasp the magnitude of this city. Gosh, Camden was the very heart of the world's industry, innovation, and technology! This is where people came to shop, to work, to live, to record their music, and to listen to it!

My neck begins to hurt from looking down at the river, so I look up at the amazing blue structure of the bridge.

50

"Those cables must be mighty strong!" I comment.

"Oh yes," says Aunt Cora. "Those two giant cables are full of thinner wires, and if all those wires were placed end to end, they would circle the earth!"

"Yes," agrees Geraldine. "And those buildings attached to the stone towers are where the cables come in and anchor onto steel beams, which are anchored to the bedrock one hundred and thirty feet below the ground under the river."

"How did they do that?" I ask.

"Sand hogs," Cora answers.

"Wha...?" I wonder out loud.

"Sand hogs is the nickname they gave the workers who dug all the way down there with their picks and shovels," she answers. "What an incredibly hard, hot, and dark job that much have been!"

"But not wet, I hope!"

"No, at least I hope there were no leaks under there!"

We're almost stopped right here at the tippy-top of the bridge, and I see something coming towards us. In the air. It's an airplane—a biplane, actually, which is an airplane with two sets of wings—towing a bright red banner behind it, with giant white words, **See the Sesqui by Air!**

"EMORY!" screams Aunt Cora! *"THAT'S MY BROTHER EMORY!"*

"You're amazing, Cora," says Geraldine. "No matter where we go, you know absolutely everybody!"

Now Uncle Emory, I've heard about. Lots. He's a family legend. Emory Conrad Malick was the first licensed black pilot, he was the first aviator to fly over central Pennsylvania back in 1911, he was the first African American pilot to earn a Federal Transport License in 1927, he was declared a hero in Camden for saving the day during an airshow in 1928, and...oh yes, he was my great-great-grandmother's and my Aunt Cora's brother.

And there he is waving to me RIGHT NOW!!!!

"Gerry, can you make a U-turn?" Aunt Cora sounds flustered, which is unlike her. I mean, not that I've known her for a long time or anything; but, so far, she strikes me as being pretty cool and collected. Not now.

"Hardly, my dear!" huffs Geraldine. "If you haven't noticed, we're stuck in traffic on the middle of a humongous bridge, miles in the air, and none of the other drivers are even watching the road—they're all gaping at your daredevil of a brother!"

Aunt Cora, however, looks very determined. She reaches for her infamous wart.

Wheee!

"What in the world just happened?" exclaims our famous celebrity. "Suddenly we're heading in the opposite direction, right back into Jersey! *Impossible!!*"

"Atta girl, Gerry! My dear, that was an absolutely ducky U-turn! I knew you could do it! What a fantastically swell driver you've become!" Aunt Cora's grinning from ear to ear—and having a grand old time with the flapper lingo, I might add.... "And look at that—somehow you're even avoiding all this utterly annoying traffic. We'll be at the Crescent Airport in no time at all—I bet we'll even beat Emory!"

"Um," I add. "I have a funny feeling we'll be arriving at the airport at just about the same time."

"Why do you say that?" asks Aunt Cora.

"Look straight up," I answer.

"HA!" shouts Gerry. "There he is, flying right above us! My dear Cora, your brother is almost as mischievous as you are!" She reaches over my head to give Cora a poke in her curls.

"How kind of him to escort us," counters my laughing aunt. "And don't go looking up in the air again. You're supposed to be driving, remember?" Although, at this point, I have a funny feeling that Aunt Cora's wart is doing most of the driving....

"Oh, Cora, don't be a worry wart." Ooh, that was kind of an insensitive comment, considering. But, then again, maybe...just maybe…Gerry doesn't even see Cora's gimungous magic wart at all…hmmm. "I'm being careful enough," continues Gerry, "but thank goodness Emory's a little bit ahead of us now. By the way, how much farther is it?"

"Not far at all," answers Aunt Cora, as we exit the bridge and keep on going.

"In any event, I should probably continue driving all the way to New York City after I drop you two off. I have a performance there tomorrow, and I'll need my beauty sleep tonight." Geraldine looks sad. "But Cora, please keep in touch. Let's not wait another lifetime before getting together again!"

Aunt Cora nods in agreement, saying, "Thank you, Gerry, again and again and again for your splendid recital today. This day is a gift to be savored always and forever."

"Yes, Miss Farrar," I add. "Thank you!"

"You're both so very welcome, my dears. This day has been a gift for me as well." Gerry continues, "And Cora, darling, I want you to promise to join me for a shopping spree next time I'm in Camden. You too, Jenna. Ah applesauce! Is this ever the best place for shopping! Let's go to Pinsky's department store and Munger and Long. They're both on Broadway, so I'll reserve a room at the new Hotel Walt Whitman on Broadway and Cooper. I usually stay at the Robeson Hotel when I come here to the recording studios, since it's on 2nd and Penn, right by the Victor Talking Machine Company, but this time the sole purpose of my visit will be to shop, have a leisurely lunch, and enjoy your delightful company."

"It's a date!" giggles Cora. "And I'd love to see a show at the new Stanley Theatre on Broadway and Market. I hear it's the largest motion picture house in the world!" she adds. "I'm sure they'll be showing your films there—I especially love *Carmen*. What a brilliant actress you are, Gerry! I just wish Eldridge would hurry up and perfect the 'talkies.' I so want to actually hear your voice when I watch you on the silver screen!"

Grandma Butch told me that her father used to play piano for the silent films back in the twenties and early thirties; but I can't say that out loud, since Geraldine probably wouldn't quite be able to fathom the fact that I actually live in the 21st century….

—

"Plus," adds Aunt Cora, "I hear that, for one quarter, you can take in a five-act stage show *and* a double feature!"

"How nifty!" exclaims Gerry. "Hey, girlfriends, we'll don our glad rags and get our wiggle on!"

"Ha, you slay me, Gerry!" says Cora. "You know, Camden is truly the cat's meow," she adds, giving me a little squeeze. Then, "Look, we're here!" We've just driven around the new Airport Circle, the very first traffic circle in the country. In 1929 the airfield will be expanded to become Camden Central Airport, the main airport for the whole Philadelphia region for twelve more years!

I watch Emory circling for a landing over there to our left as Geraldine pulls her Stutz Bearcat up on the lawn and parks next to several other cars. Aunt Cora and I climb out, hollering *"Thank You, Gerry!"* and throwing lots of kisses as she drives off toward Manhattan, waving, her green polka-dotted scarf dancing in the wind.

We watch Emory make a perfect landing, then run over to greet him. He and Cora hug as if they haven't seen each other in years. Oh, that's right, they haven't. It's hard to get used to magic, even when it keeps on happening!

Uncle Emory walks over to me with a smile and open arms. He looks as nice and as handsome as his photograph, which hangs on my grandmas' studio wall. My eyes fill with tears, in spite of myself, and I return his bear hug, and then some. I feel like I've known him forever; after all, I've been hearing stories about him my whole life. He holds me out at arm's length.

"Just look at you, Jenna—you've got Malick written all over your face. How marvelous to finally meet my fantabulous niece!" I see tears in Uncle Emory's eyes too. "You know, I don't want to say goodbye right away, but I'm here to fuel up and take off for Gettysburg. I've got to pick up a new biplane there and fly it back for the festivities tomorrow and then, on the next day, Sunday, President Coolidge will be dedicating the new bridge and planting a tree to commemorate it right here in Camden! This old machine is on its last legs, and I'm starting to get lots of customers who want to see all these Sesqui festivities from up in the air, so I need that new plane."

He studies Aunt Cora and me for a moment, rubbing his chin. "Hmmm. Any chance you two can join me for the trip? It's getting late, so we can toot on up to Sunbury and check in on the family overnight before heading back to Camden early tomorrow morning. I hear Aunt Alice has been pretty ill.

"Whattaya say, Cora and Jenna? Will you come with me?"

14. Up in the Air!

Aunt Cora looks worried. "I'd love to come along dearest brother; you know I would. It's just that...." She pauses. "Emory, why don't you go fuel up your plane while we think it over?"

As Emory nods and starts to walk over to his biplane, she brushes at her nose, as if a gnat had just landed on it, but I know she's really tapping her wart. Suddenly I hear her voice inside my head. *Jenna. I want you to go along with your great-great-great uncle, but I'm feeling a little funny. I think I might not be able to keep you here much longer.*

Well then, I respond silently, *I'll stay here with you. You can send me back to 2016 right away!*

Oh no. This would be the chance of a lifetime for you to get to know your Uncle Emory. I think I can do it, if I stay back here with Glinda to help me. She's a powerful little kitty.

You THINK? You don't know for sure? I ask, perplexed.

I don't know for sure, because...I've never done this before, she admits. *But,* she adds quickly, *I feel like I can safely hold you here in the year 1926 until...sundown tomorrow night. Emory says you'll be heading back tomorrow morning, so you'll be here in plenty of time.*

I'm having some doubts, I say, worried.

It's OK, she assures me, smiling. *Let's DO this!*

"All done!" declares Uncle Emory, returning with a grin. "You're joining me, right?" he pleads.

"Well, Emory," begins Cora. "I'd like to, more than anything in the world, but I'm feeling a little bit under the weather today. "Jenna, on the other hand, would *love* to join you!"

"Alright then!" smiles Emory. "But Cora, are you sure you'll be OK?"

"Yes, indeed!" she smiles back. "I think I ate one too many tea sandwiches this afternoon, that's all." Inside my head, she adds, *Jenna, if you need to talk to me, just tap your nose three times, and I'll hear you.*

OK, I answer. *One more thing... I don't think this fancy flapper costume would be the best flying outfit...*

Aunt Cora grins broadly. As Uncle Emory turns away to lead me over to the plane, she reaches for her wart. *Presto! How's that?* I look down and see that I'm dressed just like the famous African American aviatrix, Bessie Coleman, with jodhpurs, fancy laced-up leather boots, a long-sleeved white shirt with a black tie, heavy leather jacket, helmet and goggles, plus a wool scarf for good measure.

Thank you, Aunt Cora! But...it's July, and kind of too hot for all this.

Just you wait, my dear, until you're way up there in the sky. You'll be grateful for the warm clothes!

"Just look at you, Jenna—all dressed for the occasion!" exclaims Uncle Emory, turning around. "Cora, you're always prepared for anything!" He kisses her on the cheek, gives her a tight squeeze, then lifts me up on the bottom wing so I can climb into his biplane. I get comfortable in the front seat and fasten my seatbelt, while he walks around to the nose of the plane and starts to wind up the propeller. Yipes! I hope I don't take off without him! Remember, I've heard stories about Uncle Emory—I know that his plane, with passengers inside, once careened across a field while he ran to catch up with it back during his barnstorming days...which would be *now*, come to think of it. But no, he's climbing into the pilot's seat behind me, and starting to work the controls. We're rolling forward. *OMG, this is so exciting!* I've travelled in giant airliners all the way across the country to California to visit my cousins, Brenna and Jonah, who are almost five, and Lila, who's almost my age, but it's not the same thing as being in an open-air cockpit. No, it's not the same thing at all!

"*Yippee!!*" I holler as we start to take off. I turn to wave goodbye to Aunt Cora, but she's not there. Not anywhere at all! It's as if she ... disappeared. I tap my nose three times. *Are you OK?* I ask.

Yes, my darling Jenna. I'm fine, and so is little Glinda. Enjoy the ride!

———

58

15. Bird's Eye View

Uncle Emory starts to bank the plane to the left, and I can see all of Camden up ahead, as we slowly circle the airfield. I know that on March 4, 1928, less than two years from now, Uncle Emory will save the day right here when his engine "cronks" (dies) at an air show. He'll manage to bank the biplane and glide into a crash-landing on an empty field, avoiding all the spectators and their cars right underneath him, while saving the lives of his two passengers and himself. Not an easy task. His poor plane, however, will crumple like it was "smitten by the fist of a giant," and his passengers will have some cuts and one will have three broken ribs. But to say it could have been much worse would be a gross understatement. Hundreds of folks were looking straight up at him when the engine cronked. The newspapers will praise his skill as a pilot, calling him a "crank" on air safety—in other words, a stickler—and they'll report that he was "one of the real pioneers of the air," and they'll call him a hero, because he was. Is.

And right now I'm right here with Uncle Emory, and he's flying me in his airplane. *Unreal!*

OK, I'm pulling my goggles down, because of the wind, and because I don't want any bugs in my eyes. Now I just have to remember to keep my mouth shut...although, like usual, I have something to say, so I open it again.

"Wow, Uncle Emory! There's the Nipper Building where my grandmothers live!" Whoops. I shouldn't have said that.

"That's so strange!" answers Uncle Emory. "I thought I heard you speaking, but I usually can't hear anything my passengers say from back here. Then again, funny things always start to happen whenever I see my sister Cora. What was that you said, Jenna?"

"I said, "There's the Nipper Building where Victrolas are made!" Gosh, that didn't even rhyme with what I said before....

"Yes!" he says. Whew, he didn't notice. It's awesome to see the Nipper Building surrounded by all those other Victor buildings. How many did GB tell me there were? I'm pretty sure she said thirty-eight. There's Building #2 where the recital was today!

"And look over there to the left at those spires and that bright revolving beacon," yells out Uncle Emory. "You can see that light from thirty miles away! It sits on top of the Van Sciver Company, the largest furniture plant in the whole U. S. of A. Do you see the size of that building? It's right down there at Delaware and Federal Streets, and takes up ten whole acres!"

"Yes! It's huge—but so is just about everything down there." I'm looking at the Campbell Soup Company, the Victor complex, and New York Ship.

"They build and sell the furniture all in the same place. Customers come here from all over, from Philadelphia and New York, plus all the thousands of folks who've moved here to Camden to work. Eldridge Johnson got his idea for the Victrola cabinets right there at Van Sciver's. He wanted them to look like elegant pieces of furniture, not just pieces of equipment. His cabinets were designed by Miss Virginia Hamill of New York."

"I smell coffee!" I yell, as we circle around over the waterfront.

"Smells good, huh? That would be coming from Scull Coffee Company right down there at Front and Federal. I declare, Jenna, Camden is the center of the world when it comes to business and technology. It even has several cigar companies!" *Pee Yew*, I'm thinking. Thank goodness, I've only ever smelled a cigar one time. That was more than enough....

"Right below us is the Camden Theatre, at Fourth and Market. And swimming pools! There are three giant swimming pools, four recreation centers and twelve playgrounds here. Sometimes I wish I lived right here in Camden, and not over in Philly! Although, hmm...Philly's swell too. Speaking of Philly, how about we fly over the Sesqui grounds? I'll give you the tour!"

"Yay! I'd love to!" I cry out. The wind feels so alive and happy on my smiling cheeks. I look down and see that we're crossing over the Delaware River. Right behind us is the giant Pennsylvania Railroad Station on Camden's waterfront. And look over there at the skyline of Philadelphia! City Hall, with Willy Penn's statue, is the tallest building, just like in the olden days. Oh, that's right...this IS the olden days! Below us we can see the ferry boats, tugboats, and gigantic ships on the river. The new bridge looks majestic.

A seagull is flying right next to me.

16. The Sesqui

"Ya know, Jenna," yells Uncle Emory, "I think I'll just circle around the city, so you can see where I live, right over at 19th and Mount Vernon Street." First we fly over Independence Hall and the Betsy Ross House. Now I feel like I can reach out my hand and pat Willie Penn on his hat!

"How come you can fly so low?" I ask.

"I sure won't be able to next year at this time!" he laughs. "The U.S. government has finally decided to regulate air travel. The Air Commerce Act of 1926 just passed in May, and the new Aeronautics Branch of the Department of Commerce will be opening next month. I've been informed that I'll have to apply for a Federal Transport License in order to continue flying passengers, and they'll start issuing them next year, 1927. Soon there'll be a lot more rules to follow; but, on the other hand, flying should become much safer, once it's regulated by our government. I had to pass a test in order to qualify for my International Pilot's License back in 1912, but pilots aren't required to have that license in order to fly; so, I'm afraid there are a few so-called pilots up here in the sky who have no idea what they're doing!"

"So if it's safer, you'll get more passengers, right?" I ask, knowing that Uncle Emory will, in fact, be the very first black pilot to earn a Federal Transport License. James Herman Banning will be the first African American aviator to earn a Federal Limited Commercial License, and Phoebe Fairgrave Omlie will be the first woman to earn a Federal Transport License, all in 1927.

"Yes, indeed!" he answers. I can hear his smile. "Flying Dutchman Air Service will be even busier for Ernie Buehl and me every weekend, I hope, and I'll keep on working with Vic Dallin out of Pine Valley Airport in Jersey and Virgil Kauffman of the Aero Service Corp here in Philly, with the aerial photography business, and there will be more air shows in Camden. Very exciting!

"Aviation is my passion, you know," he adds. "I'm also a carpenter, a master tile-layer, and an airplane mechanic, but I prefer to spend my time in the air, whenever possible.

"Oh Jenna, look where I'm pointing, there's the boarding house where I live! I've boarded at several different houses on Mount Vernon Street over the years, not far from where the new Philadelphia Museum of Art is being built. The museum site's right over there by the Water Works on the Schuylkill River. Isn't it fabulous? Memorial Hall has been our art museum for the past fifty years, since the Centennial Celebration, but this is even better—such a huge space, and what a gorgeous location!"

We circle over the river. The scene with Boathouse Row, the river, the trees, and lots of sculls and their rowers, is so beautiful. My Aunt Suzannah would be rowing there for Lower Merion High School in the 1990s. We're low enough to catch a whiff of summer flowers, then we're off to the Sesqui.

"We'll just head back to Willie Penn and fly south, right down Broad Street," says Uncle Emory. "Wait till you see!"

I don't really know what I expected. Maybe a fair ground with a Ferris wheel and a merry-go-round? But the scene below us is…*WOW!* The Sesquicentennial International Exposition of 1926 is humongous! It covers the whole area where the stadiums are now, plus so much more. The gateway to the fair spans Broad Street, a couple of blocks north of Packer Avenue, and consists of a giant, eighty-foot-tall replica of the Liberty Bell, which shines like the sun. Uncle Emory says it's lit up with 26,000 light bulbs!

"Look, Jenna, there's Treasure Island!" he announces with pride. "It's a children's paradise!" I agree. I see the Rocky Mountains, a miniature railroad, a giant sliding board…

"Over there!" he points to the right. "There's Robinson Crusoe's Beach, with a pirate's lair, and you can take boat rides. And there's Noah's Ark, complete with animals!" We circle back, and I see a tower of light, surrounded by several buildings and gardens. The famous architect Louis Kahn helped design the buildings back when he was just starting out. There are plenty of rides, but this is all on a much larger scale than I ever could have imagined, and it extends all the way down to the Navy Yard on the Delaware River.

"You know, President Coolidge will be speaking here on Sunday for the official Grand Opening of the Sesquicentennial, then he'll be visiting Independence Hall before heading on over to Camden. It's going to be a big day for my 'See the Sesqui by Air' promotion. In other words, I'm thinking we'll have one more go-round, then we'd better head on out to Gettysburg, before it gets too late. We want to be in Sunbury before dark, then back here tomorrow morning!" We circle around over the Municipal Stadium, where I see lots of spectators watching a rodeo…and, lo and behold, all the riders are women!

"That one looks like Ruth Roach!" yells Uncle Emory. "I can tell by her giant hair bows. She's one famous cowgirl!"

"Yippee Yi-Yo, Ki-Yay!" I sing at the top of my lungs, as we circle around one more time, and then head west.

Here we go, into the wild blue yonder! I'm singing to myself as Uncle Emory flies us up and away from Philly. *Westward ho!* I look down to see the Pennsylvania Turnpike, but it's simply not there yet…something tells me the landscape has certainly changed a lot over the past ninety years! I see lots of countryside and, way down below, a field of cows, and there's a horse and buggy on a tiny road. There goes a Pierce Arrow! I know my cars because of Grandma Butch—she can identify just about anything on wheels. Not Buckadee, though. She can tell you if a car is red or white or a mini-van or a convertible, and that's about it. We keep climbing upward as we speed along to Gettysburg. There are a few puffy clouds nearby, but the sky's mostly blue. The glaring sun is starting to sink toward the west, which is where we're headed, so I close my eyes, take a deep breath of cold air, try to relax, and tap my nose three times.

How are you feeling, Aunt Cora?

Still doing OK, my dear. I'm sipping some tea and Glinda is playing with her ribbon, while we listen to Gerry's latest recording. But please don't dawdle coming back to me tomorrow morning. How are YOU doing? How's your trip so far?

Fantastically awesome! Now we're way up high in the sky, and thank you for the warm clothes—it's downright freezin' up here!

HA! I told you so!

Aunt Cora, I have a question…

Yes, Jenna?

Should I say something to Uncle Emory about those two crashes I know he's going to have in 1928? The one in Camden when his engine dies and he saves the day by crash landing away from all the spectators? And then the one in Woodbury when his plane nose-dives in the swamp and his passenger is killed and Uncle Emory can no longer fly because of his terrible injuries? Can I stop these horrible crashes from happening?

Oh Jenna, my love. I'm sorry to say that the things that have already happened are written in stone. We can open windows in the present by shining a bright light on the people and events that have come before us, but we can't change them. And, anyway, even if you were to say something to your Uncle Emory...well, how do you think he'd respond?

Hmm. He'd probably look at me and shake his head. He'd be disappointed that I'm so childish as to think I can predict the future. And he'd think I'm a Negative Nancy to warn him about being careful two years in advance.... He'd probably think I'd be doubting his abilities as an expert aviator—one of the best in the world—and that would make him sad. Right?

So right, my beloved Astute One.

I kind of figured as much, but I thought I'd better ask, just in case... Anyhow, thank you, Aunt Cora. Oh my, we're starting to descend already!

OK, my dear, we'll sign off for now. Hold on tight!

I will. I love you, Aunt Cora.

I love you too, Jenna.

We come in for a perfect landing…hardly even a bounce, which is pretty good, considering we're on a field, and not concrete. Uncle Emory taxis over until we're near the hangar, then he parks our plane and turns off the engine. I see three other biplanes parked outside and notice a man standing next to one. Uncle Emory climbs out, then lifts me to the ground. *Whoo!* I'm a little wobbly. It takes me a minute to get my land-legs. Uncle Emory waves to the man, and starts to walk over toward him. I follow. The man doesn't wave back. He just stands there, looking at my uncle and not smiling.

"Simon!" calls Uncle Emory. "Are you the Simon I spoke with on the phone?" The man just stands there, scowling.

"My name's Simon," he spits out, as if he has a bad taste in his mouth.

"Well, hello then. I'm Emory Malick. I spoke with you the other day about trading in this old tin can for your Waco 9."

"It's not for sale," spits Simon.

"What do you mean, it's not for sale?" asks Uncle Emory, looking worried.

"Just lak' I said."

Uncle Emory looks at him for a moment, then says, "But you assured me over the phone, Simon, that you were all set to sell me this airplane. We even settled on a price. It's a done deal."

Simon looks mean. I see four white men appear around the side of the hangar, walking toward us. "That was before I saw your face!" he spits out. "I only sell to white folks, not coloreds." Now he's looking *really* nasty. His face has turned somewhere between red and purple. Magenta? And he's suddenly spewing ugly curses at Emory that I can't even begin to understand—and I've heard some pretty nasty swear words in my day.

Well, now *I'm* getting mad too. Nobody talks like that to my uncle!

"Hey, buddy, NICE MOUTH!" I shout. I'm shaking real hard, but I can't shut up. *"Do you EAT with that thing?"* Simon takes a step toward me as Uncle Emory swoops me up in his arms and carries me away in a hurry.

"Emory! Emory Malick!" shouts one of the four men who had been walking over toward us.

"Jack! Jack Spaid, Harry Neidig, J. B. McCalley and Johnny Abusio! I can't believe it!" laughs Uncle Emory, putting me back down, and breathing a sigh of relief. Yeah, me too. I take a real deep breath, because I wasn't breathing at all, I don't think. I was mad and scared all at the same time.

Simon's eyes open wide, and he swivels around and skulks away into the hangar.

It turns out that all four gentlemen are fellow barnstormers from central Pennsylvania who all know and love Uncle Emory. In the 1980s, Jack Spaid will give a talk and write a nice article about Emory being the very first aviator to fly over central Pennsylvania. J. B. McCalley got his license with Uncle Emory out in San Diego back in 1912 at the Curtiss School of Aviation, and they performed in air shows together. Johnny Abusio was a barnstormer who actually taught my great grandmother Charlotte Howell how to fly! And Harry Neidig's a friend who, in a couple of years, will try to talk Emory into riding along with him in his plane after that final crash in 1928. Emory won't do it, saying, "I had my fun and now I'm done." What a heartbreak that must have been for Uncle Emory to let go of his dream, right when he was becoming so successful in his chosen field. Aviation. His passion.

"So Emory," says Jack. "What just happened with that fellow Simon? Sounded like trouble."

Emory explains what happened, and they all frown deeply. "The guy's a bigoted jerk," announces Harry. "But he owns the plane, so I'm guessing we can't force him to sell it."

"Hey, Jenna! You are one brave little girl, defending your uncle like that!" gushes Jack. "I was sure you were gonna deck that guy right in the nose!" I stand here and look at him. I can't find my voice just yet, and the hair's still standing up on the back of my neck.

"That miserable Simon is probably a member of the Klan," adds Johnny. "That's a big deal here in Pennsylvania, I'm sorry to say." Yes, Buckadee told me once that the racist Ku Klux Klan was—and still is—bigger in Pennsylvania than anywhere else in the country, even Alabama. Disgusting.

"Yup," says Uncle Emory, nodding his head. "Ya know, I'm real glad you guys showed up. Things could have gotten extremely ugly."

"Yeah, I'm glad we're here too," says Jack. "We'll help you gas up your plane while we try to think of a solution."

"Wait, I know what you can do!" exclaims J. B. "There's a nice fellow who has an airstrip right in Harrisburg, over at 14th and Sycamore Streets. He also owns the Automobile and Aeroplane Mechanical School on Cameron Street."

"Yeah, I heard about him too," adds Johnny. "And I understand he's selling a Waco 9!"

"I heard the same," says J. B. "His name is William McDonald Felton, and he's the same color as you are, Emory, so there shouldn't be a problem!"

"Oh, what a relief," sighs Uncle Emory. "I really need a new plane. Thanks guys," he says, shaking each of their hands in turn. "Well, come on now, Jenna, let's go to Harrisburg and buy us a Waco 9! We don't wanna give that mean ol' Simon our money, anyhoo, do we?" He looks at me and sees that I'm still a bit shaky, so he picks me up, hugs me tight, then lifts me up on the wing so I can climb in.

Yup! It's back into the wild blue yonder for us!

19. The Feltons

"Bessie Coleman was right," says Uncle Emory, soon after we take off.

"What do you mean?"

"She said, 'The air is the only place free of prejudices.' She was right. Maybe that's why I love flying so much," he says with a sigh. "Today wasn't the first time I've run into trouble because of prejudice. And I suspect it won't be the last. I'm just really, really sorry that you got pulled into that nasty situation, Jenna."

"Don't apologize, Uncle Emory. It wasn't your fault!" I say because it's true. "That guy was horrible."

"Yes, he was. Tell me why, oh why, are some people like that? They think they're better than anyone who doesn't look like them and think like them, or have as much money as they do, or have more money than they do. You name it, they'll hate you for it. It's just sad."

"Yes, it is," I answer. "The way I see it, Uncle Emory, I'm just grateful that I am who I am, and that I'm not small-minded like they are. Think how awful it would be to be like that!"

"You're a wise child, for sure, Jenna. Thank you for giving me a better perspective on the subject. In the future I'll just feel sorry for ignorant people like Simon—but I won't stick around to tell them about it, and I sure as heck won't do business with them, either!"

"What's that round building over yonder, Uncle Emory?" I ask.

"Good eye, Jenna! That's the Capitol Building in Harrisburg. My father and I helped build that building twenty years ago. Artists are still working on the mural in the Supreme Court Chambers. I can't wait to see it! The Capitol is well worth visiting, if I do say so myself. The dome is spectacular, especially when you go inside the building and look up at it.

"Now look down to the left! There's the Pennsylvania Railroad station, just like in Camden and Philadelphia. In fact, the Pennsy is the largest railroad in the whole country! Your Grandpa Darius and I also helped put the mahogany veneering in their dining and sleeping cars, right here in Harrisburg." Actually, Uncle Emory's dad was my great-great-great grandfather, but 'mum's the word'

71

right now. I don't want to upset the apple cart. I'm learning. Sometimes it's good to be an apple-cart-upsetter, but other times— maybe not so much.

"There it is—the landing strip J. B. McCalley told us about. We're heading down for a landing, Jenna. Time for another adventure!" It looks pretty small for an airfield; but, once again, Emory pulls off a perfect landing, and taxis over to the hangar.

As Uncle Emory is lifting me down, a very stylish woman strides over to us.

"Hello!" she greets us. "My name is Josephine Souza Felton, and I own this airfield with my husband, William McDonald Felton. How may we help you today?"

Uncle Emory introduces us, then says, "It's a pleasure to meet you, Mrs. Felton! I'm sad to say I hadn't heard about your operation before today. But here we are now, and we're looking to buy a Waco 9. We were just told by Mr. J. B. McCalley that you might have one for sale."

"You've come to the right place!" we hear from a jovial gentleman, who turns out to be Mr. Felton. He reaches out his hand in greeting as he walks over from the hangar to join us. The three of them bicker and haggle for a time, in a very friendly fashion, then Mrs. Felton walks into the hangar and soon, after revving the engine, drives the sparkling new airplane out into the sunshine.

"She's all yours!" she announces with panache. It looks like Uncle Emory is trying really hard not to actually jump for joy, so I do it for him.

"Yippee!" I shout. "What a beautiful plane!" They all laugh at my antics. Then I turn to Mrs. Felton. "You're a pilot?"

"Yes, indeed," she answers, as she jumps back down to the ground. "I'm very proud to be a black woman pilot, or aviatrix, especially now that we've just lost—on April 30—our Queen Bess." I see tears in her eyes.

"Oh yes," we all agree.

"Our Bessie Coleman was taken from us at the height of her career," adds Mr. Felton.

"Sabotage," says Mrs. Felton. "There's no doubt about it. Some folks just don't want us up in the air."

"Or down on the ground, either," adds Uncle Emory with a shrug.

——

72

"It was because of her success," adds Mrs. Felton. "Mark my words. That's all I'm gonna say."

"My wife Josephine, I must add, has been flying since…before 1919, and is, by my calculations, actually the very first black aviatrix in the world!" boasts Mr. Felton proudly.

"And," adds Mrs. Felton, "I hear there's a Mr. Charles Wesley Peters out in Pittsburgh who's also a black aviator. He flew his homemade glider in 1906, and then built an engine-powered plane, which he also flew successfully."

"My goodness gracious!" exclaims Uncle Emory.

"Please, join us for dinner!" says Mr. Felton. "We've got so much to talk about!"

"Oh my, we would love to spend more time with you," responds Uncle Emory. "However, we need to get up to Sunbury before nightfall, and I'm starting to see a little pink in the sky, so we'd better head on out. But we'll definitely take a rain check on that dinner! And please come visit when you get to the Philadelphia and Camden area. I'll cook for you myself," promises Uncle Emory with a grin.

He hoists me up on the bottom wing of our new biplane, and I climb in. I love it! It's like getting a gigantic new toy!

Uncle Emory starts up the engine with one turn of the propeller, climbs in, and we're off into the sunset!

We both turn and wave to our new friends.

"Oh, Uncle Emory! *Magnifico!*" There's something about being up in the air to really appreciate the perfect sunset. By now we're well on our way, with Uncle Emory doing some dips and turns to try out his new purchase. *Wheee!* At around sixty to seventy miles an hour, we'll be there in no time. Sunbury's only about forty-five miles north of Harrisburg. We're flying fairly low over the Susquehanna River, and the reflection of the rosy sky in the water, surrounded by lush forest, is breathtaking. We're high enough for the air to be crisp and clear, not hot and humid. I just caught a whiff of honeysuckle. Yum. Ya gotta love the summertime. I'm grinning from ear to ear, even if it means I might swallow a high-flying mosquito, or maybe even a dragonfly! But now I'm cringing again.

"Uncle Emory?"

"Yes, Jenna?"

"I'm sorry."

"Whatever for?"

"For losing my temper this afternoon, and maybe putting us in danger."

"It's OK, honey. I was mad too. Sometimes it's impossible not to just go ballistic when somebody pushes all your buttons like that. I was proud that you stood up for me."

"You were?" I ask, incredulous.

"Of course!" he laughs. "*Holey Moley,* it's not every day someone lashes out at a nasty ol' son of a gun who's twice her size and meaner than a hornet, all on my account!"

"You're the best uncle in the world, you know that?"

"I must be, for you to watch out for me like that! Or maybe it's just that you're the best niece in the world."

I'm laughing, but still wincing a bit. "I still think what I did was stupid, and I'm sorry. I'll try to control my temper from now on—especially when it's safer to hold it in!"

"You have a point. Sometimes lashing out can make matters worse." He thinks for a moment. "On the other hand, I believe we can use our anger to make the world a better place. It can motivate us to change the things that anger us."

"That makes sense."

"Ya know something, Jenna?"

"No, what?"

"You're a good girl, and I love you very much."

"I love you too, Uncle Emory." All of a sudden I see that the shadows are lengthening, the wind has died down, and the calm river looks like a shiny mirror from up here. My eyelids are starting to feel real heavy. After all, it's been quite a day, don't you agree? *Yawn.*

"Prepare for landing!" announces Uncle Emory. And then we do. Good. I'm looking forward to a bite to eat, a soft bed, and a good night's sleep. "And not a minute too soon," he adds, since it's starting to get pretty dark. We land smoothly on the long, green field.

"But look—we're in luck! *Hey, Sam!*" he hollers. I see a man who was just about to get in his car. A sky-blue Packard.

"Emory Malick, the Birdman! What are you doing here, old fella!"

"We just flew all the way from Camden so you could give us a ride over to the house!" answers Uncle Emory.

"Ha!" says Sam. "You're just in time, then! Nice plane!"

"Thanks," says Emory. "We just picked it up in Harrisburg. Sam, I'd like you to meet my niece Jenna. Jenna, this is Sam McCarty, an old friend and a member of the Sunbury Flying Club."

"Nice car!" I say, and he smiles broadly as we shake hands.

"We're here for the night," Emory tells him, as we climb in the Packard, "then back to the Sesqui celebration tomorrow morning."

We're on the airfield on Island Park in Sunbury, an island nestled in the Susquehanna River right between Northumberland and the rest of Sunbury. It's a short drive across the bridge and over to the Malick house on Catawissa Avenue.

When we pull up to the house, it's almost completely dark. After we climb out of the car and say goodbye to Mr. McCarty, I notice the sound of crickets chirping and see lots of lightning bugs flying around. I reach out and catch one in my hand, then set it free again. It flashes its tiny light in gratitude.

"I hear a violin playing!" I say.

"No, that would be my father's viola. It's like a violin but a little bigger. And the music's coming from next door, at Aunt

Alice's. Let's go over there." We walk up to the screen door and my uncle knocks lightly. The music stops, and Darius Malick tiptoes over to let us in.

"Shhh!" he whispers as we walk inside. He hugs us both. "Alice just fell asleep. She always drifts off when I play my viola. Laura and I have set up a bed for her right over here in the living room, so we can keep an eye on her. She's not doing very well, I'm afraid." Laura runs in from the kitchen and hugs her big brother.

"It's so good to see you, Emory!" she whispers.

"I've missed you, Sis. It's wonderful that you could be here to help with Aunt Alice," he whispers back. Laura turns to me, and I get a hug too. I've heard about these relatives from Buckadee, so I feel like I know them; but they also seem to know me, so I have a feeling Aunt Cora's been tapping her wart again. Laura and Darius whisk Emory off to the kitchen so they can bring him up to date on Alice's condition. I hear murmurs that she's "senile," "out of her mind," "makes absolutely no sense," "crazy as a loon," not to mention "sick as a dog," and "not long for this world, I'm sad to say."

Suddenly I see her. Aunt Alice. My eyes are adjusting to the low light, and I realize I'm standing right beside her bed. She's light-skinned but clearly black, just like Uncle Emory and me. I notice that she also has a slightly green hue…she must be pretty darn sick. In fact, she's lying there so stiff and still that I'm afraid that she's already expired. I lean in closer to make sure she's still breathing. All of a sudden her eyes pop open!

"Jenna," she hisses. *"I know all about you and Cora!"*

I just almost wet my pants.

Aunt Laura tiptoes into the room, whispering, "Jenna, what a terrible hostess I am. You must be starving! I've cooked up a nice stew with vegetables from the garden and made some cornbread. Come on in the kitchen!" Aunt Alice looks like she's fast asleep again, as if nothing just happened. Nothing at all. I ask Aunt Laura if I can use the bathroom, and I get there just in time. Now for some chow!

While I'm gobbling my second hunk of cornbread, Aunt Laura says, "Jenna, I'm afraid we're short on beds, since we're all staying here to care for Alice. Would you mind sleeping on the sofa in the living room? I'll make it all comfy for you, with sheets and a pillow. If you get chilly, you can snuggle under the afghan, but it's pretty warm out, so you probably won't need it. Alice usually sleeps peacefully through the night, and she never snores, so you should be fine." I grab my glass of water, because I seem to be having trouble swallowing my cornbread.

"Are you OK, Jenna?" asks Grandpa.

"Yes, I'm fine," I choke.

Emory says, "Well, we'd better turn in soon, since we'll be off bright and early in the morning. I wish you two could come back with us and see the Sesqui, but it looks like that's out of the question, what with Aunt Alice so sick."

"Yup," says Grandpa. "It's a shame she's suffering so. I wish we could come back with you too, son. It sounds like Philadelphia is the place to be these days!"

"Camden too!" I add. "President Coolidge is going to plant a tree there on Monday!"

"How exciting!" says Aunt Laura. "I hope the weather holds!"

"Ok, little one," says Uncle Emory as he walks over and kisses me on the head. "Time to turn in. I'll wake you up at daybreak, and we'll head on back to the big city in our fancy new contraption."

Aunt Laura offers me a much too large nightgown, but it's nice and soft. I glance over at Aunt Alice as I snuggle under the sheet. The others tread softly and slowly up the stairs to their beds. I dare to close my eyes. The crickets are singing outside the window behind my sofa. A cool breeze is wafting through the screen.

Smells like summer. I think about all that happened on this day of days. I wonder about my grandmas. I wonder about Aunt Cora. I think I'll reach up and tap my nose....

"*Psst! Jenna!*" Uh oh. Aunt Alice is awake. I open my eyes and see a pulsating green glow emanating from her. I close my eyes and open them again. Yup, it's still there. I look up to see if there's a green spotlight on the ceiling. No, no spotlight. Or maybe the glow is coming from the full moon shining through the maple leaves. Nope, it's definitely coming from her.

"*Come here, Jenna.*" Ok, I'm officially scared. But, instead of hightailing it out the door or up the stairs, I feel my bare feet on the cool wooden floor, padding obediently over to her. I look down at her very wrinkly, very...green face. Her eyes are wide open again.

"*Jenna,*" she croaks. "Don't be afraid. I've been watching your whole day unfold, as if I were watching one of those newfangled TV sets that don't exist yet. As I rush closer to my death, I can see more and more clearly. I know they're saying I'm insane, but...it's because I know too much. They can't comprehend that I'm seeing the future, or traveling to different dimensions, so they assume I'm out of my mind. There's simply no context other than 'mentally unstable' for an old colored woman in the 1920s who simply knows too much. When I say things that others don't understand, they automatically figure something's wrong with me, not with them. When you go back home, check your family records and you'll see that Alice Malick died on July 10, 1926, a week from today, from dementia."

"*Oh!*" I cry out.

"It's OK, my dear. My time on earth working my knuckles off as a housemaid in this one-horse town is soon over and I'm content with that. I'm resolved to finishing out my earthly journey, discarding this sick old body, and joining your Aunt Cora in her world. Look closely, and you'll see that I'm already growing a tiny wart on the tip of my nose!" I peer closer and...thar she blows!

"Yup!" I say, then, "Aunt Alice, are you a witch? Is Aunt Cora a witch?"

"Ha!" she exclaims. "Yes indeedie! In fact, you couldn't get any witchier than we are! And it looks like you're next in line to inherit the title, Witch of Winnengen."

"Winnengen?"

"Yes, it's a town in Germany that's known for its delectable Malick wine." She pauses and studies me with her dark brown eyes that go on forever. Looking into her eyes is like staring up at the night sky. "Winnengen is also celebrated for having been the center of the witch hunts in Europe. And it's the town from whence our ancestors escaped in the 1700s, hightailing it over here to central Pennsylvania, where they could live free of prejudices."

"Were the Malick witches bad?" I ask.

"Are you bad? Is your Aunt Cora bad?"

"Oh, no! We're good people, and so are you, I presume."

"Thank you, dearie," she smiles mischievously, her dark eyes sparkling. "Well then, there you have it! We're good people who have kind hearts, special powers, and dark complexions, all of which tend to scare folks. We also have a tendency toward a certain, um, glow, because we're *green* witches."

"Green witches? I'm not green!" I exclaim.

"Your eyes are quite green," she laughs, and you do have a bit of a greenish aura about you right now. I look down at my hands. I can't tell for sure, but she might be right. Aunt Alice sees that I'm not thrilled at the thought of being green. "Mostly, my dearie, you don't look all that green, at least not yet, and maybe not much at all until you're in my condition. The main thing is this: being a green witch means you care a great deal about Mother Earth and about her children. You're sensitive to their needs and their aspirations, and you love them for who they are, no matter what stage of their journey they're enduring—or enjoying. You're a fine teacher, Jenna, and you learn a great deal from every new moment. And you can see the green."

"Wha?"

"If the rest of the family walked in here right now, they'd see me sleeping like before. No green glow. Even if you and I were flaming green like phosphorescent emeralds, no mere mortal would notice anyway." I kind of don't think she's aware of how very green she is. She looks away, and I see a tiny emerald teardrop trace across her cheek and down to her pillow. Aunt Alice continues. "Sometimes they hear me talking to Cora and assume I'm babbling nonsense, but that's because they're hearing only one side of the conversation. You, on the other hand, would see Cora, and hear both of us—and then you'd add your own two cents! Ha!"

"I'm worried about Aunt Cora."

"Yes, me too, dear. I wanted so badly to speak with you in person before I cross over next week, so I took the liberty of summoning you here today. Ya gotta admit, it was the perfect opportunity!"

"What? You summoned me?"

"Didn't you notice how surprised Cora was when Emory's airplane appeared over the bridge?"

"Heh! She sure was flustered!" I agree. "That was some U-turn!" Alice laughs, then looks serious.

"Yes, this little side-trip to Sunbury was not part of her plan. No, not at all," she says, looking guilty. "I'm afraid I didn't think to consult her before making sure you encountered Emory on top of the bridge; but...you gotta admit, it was the most scrumptious serendipity, and, well...I just couldn't help myself."

"So now what?"

"I don't know."

"You don't know?"

"No. That's why I'm afraid that I might have put you both in danger by arbitrarily extending your stay. I don't know—and Cora herself doesn't know either—how long she can keep you here in the year 1926, and what the consequences might be if she can't."

"Well, what should I do?"

"Remember what Eleanor said."

"Eleanor?" I ask, "As in Eleanor Roosevelt, our First Lady from 1933-1942, and the United States Delegate to the United Nations from 1945-1952, whom President Truman called The First Lady of the World? *That* Eleanor?"

"Yes, smarty pants! And what, pray tell, did she say to do in a situation such as this?" smirks Aunt Alice, positive she has caught me.

OK. Thinking cap on. "You must do the thing you think you cannot do."

"Say it again, Jenna."

"You must do the thing you think you cannot do."

"Jenna, WAKE UP!"

"Wha...?" Oh my, it looks pretty darn bright outside for it to be daybreak.

"I was getting worried! I've been trying to wake you up for well over an hour!" sighs Uncle Emory. "Are you OK?"

"Yes, just a little groggy." Wow.

"And who is Eleanor, and what is it you can't do?" This is weird. No one ever told me before that I talk in my sleep. Hmm...Eleanor won't be First Lady for another seven years....so I'll just gloss that part over.

"There's absolutely *nothing* I can't do!" I announce as I sit up, rub my eyes, and reach for my Bessie Coleman flying outfit. I glance over at Aunt Alice and see a smile flutter across her sleeping face.

"How about I pack up some cornbread while you get dressed?" Uncle Emory whispers loudly as he heads for the kitchen. "Laura says she'll drive us over to the airplane."

"Fine! I'll be ready in a minute," I answer as I wrestle myself out of my giant nightgown.

After a big hug from Grandpa, we head out into the sunshine. Not a cloud in the sky. I hear a drumbeat in the distance.

"Oh that's right! Happy Fourth of July!" sings out Aunt Laura.

We reach the airfield in no time, and Uncle Emory hoists me up on the bottom wing of the biplane right after we exchange quick hugs with his sister.

"Ready for takeoff!" he shouts. "We'll celebrate the Fourth of July way up high in the sky, just like the fireworks!" We circle around and fly low over the house as we head south. I wave to Grandpa, who's standing out on the front porch, waiting to see us fly over. Up the street are several kids laughing and running, and I hear the popping sound of firecrackers and cap guns. They all look up and wave.

"Uncle Emory, where did you first start flying airplanes?"

"Very close to here," he answers. "In fact, my first flight that made it into the newspapers was in an engine-powered biplane that I built myself, just south of here in Seven Points, where I was born. We're almost over the field right now. Look down to your left. That was in 1911. I also had flights near Shamokin, a few miles to the east, in 1912, the summer after I earned my International Pilot's License out in San Diego at the Curtiss School of Aviation."

"Was that the same kind of license that Bessie Coleman had?" I ask.

"Yes, it's called an FAI license, which stands for Federation Aeronautique Internationale. The international organization is based in France, where Bessie went to get her license; but, in this country, FAI licenses are issued through the Aero Club of America. My license is number 105. Eugene Bullard, another African American aviator, got his FAI license five years later, in 1917, when he was flying for France during World War I. The United States didn't allow black pilots in the military then, and they still don't." I know that black pilots wouldn't be allowed to fly until World War II, when the Tuskegee Airmen would prove themselves to be superior aviators, and, thanks to them, civil rights for all would eventually become the law of the land. Eleanor Roosevelt helped make that happen, soon after her visit to the airfield in Tuskegee in 1941, where black civilian pilots were being trained. She went up to the chief flight instructor, Mr. Charles Alfred Anderson, and told him that she had heard that "colored people" couldn't fly, but that it appeared that he could fly just fine. Then she insisted that Chief Anderson take her up for a ride in his airplane, even though her bodyguards tried to forbid her to go up with him, even frantically telephoning her husband, President Franklin Delano Roosevelt, who replied, "Well, if she wants to do it, there's nothing we can do to stop her." *Ha!*

So Chief Anderson took Mrs. Roosevelt up for a forty-minute ride that changed history! After landing, she said, "Well I see you can fly, all right!" Then she insisted that a photograph be taken of the two of them, which she sent to the White House, *pronto!* Within a short time, the 99th Pursuit Squadron, known as The Tuskegee Airmen, or the Red Tails, was created, and African American pilots were finally allowed to fly for the military, with Chief Anderson as their Chief Primary Flight Instructor.

Chief's friend, neighbor, and colleague, Roscoe Draper, also a Primary Flight Instructor for the Tuskegee Airmen, is a friend of Buckadee's, and he's ninety-seven years old now! But back in 1926, he was only seven years old. Wow.

Emory continues, "As I mentioned before, I'll be getting my Federal Transport License next year, in 1927, since I'll be required to have one in order to continue flying, and in order to carry passengers."

Uncle Emory's Flying Dutchman Air Service was operated with the help of Ernie Buehl, Emory's business partner. In 1932, after Emory no longer flew, Ernie, a pilot and mechanic from Germany, helped Chief Anderson obtain his Federal Transport License over the objections of a racist administrator who refused to give him the required flight check until Ernie said, "You're going to give him the flight check—he deserves it—he's qualified and I demand that you give him the flight check or else you're going to have to deal with me!" The man gave him the flight check, but refused to give him a score above 80% on his written test, just high enough to pass, even though Chief Anderson had earned 100%. At least Chief got his Federal Transport License. And all this happened after he had taught himself to fly in a plane that he bought with his own money, but then could find no pilot to teach him...because he was black. I consider discrimination, prejudice, hate, bigotry, racism, Jim Crow, and segregation to be curse words. Even in 2016 we have to carry signs screaming BLACK LIVES MATTER, even though we have a black President!

But now we're back in the midst of 1926....

"Did you ever crash?" I ask Uncle Emory, knowing the answer, and starting to wonder if he was ever the victim of sabotage... especially those two crashes that are destined to happen in 1928....

"Oh my, yes. I'm just glad I'm still alive to tell you the story about all my crashes! Those early airplanes—actually 'aeroplanes' was the term used back then—were very dangerous. Lethal, in fact. They were kind of like box kites with motors, and unreliable motors at that. And there I was, courageous and crazy enough to go up in one! I'm sad to say that many of my colleagues were killed. One little wind gust could plunge a flimsy plane right into the ground, and you were sitting out in the open, with absolutely no protection.

"In fact," he says slowly, "I saw one of the other Curtiss students, Rutherford Page, crash to his death at the Los Angeles Air Show, soon after I arrived in California for my training program. And we lost quite a few others around that time. Lincoln Beachey, Julia Clarke...."

"There were women pilots way back then?" I ask.

"Oh yes!" he answers. "Julia was in my Curtiss class of 1912, after being rejected by the Wright Brothers' aviation school for being a woman, as if she could help what sex she was! And there was Mrs. Atwater...oh, and Blanche Stuart Scott, whom Glenn Curtiss trained to fly back in 1910. And Harriet Quimby, who was the first woman licensed pilot in the U.S. In France, we had Marie Marvingt, who flew in 1909, and Elise Deroche, 'the Flying Baroness,' the first licensed woman pilot in the world! In Belgium there was Helene Dutrieu, the 'Woman Sparrowhawk.' Plenty of women, but plenty of discrimination, too. Even now, in 1926, women have finally been authorized by the International Commission for Air Navigation to fly commercial planes, but they're not supposed to take passengers! So how is a woman pilot to make a living, I ask you?"

"Why would anyone think that what sex you are or what color your skin is would in any way affect your ability to fly a plane?" I wonder.

"Yeah. Go figure," he says. I can hear his frown.

"Uncle Emory, tell me more about your flights!"

"Well, in the first one at Seven Points, I got up to about forty-five feet before the motor died and down I went."

"Ouch!"

"Yes, but not so bad that time. You see, I also build and fly my own gliders, so when the engine dies, I don't panic, I just keep on flying—because a crash landing sure beats a nosedive, any day! The wings still do their job, if you can manipulate the airplane to catch the air currents; as a matter of fact, I turn the engine off on purpose when I'm flying aerial photographers. If the engine's running, then the photographs will be all blurry."

"That must be scary!"

"Um, yeah, it's a bit nip 'n tuck there for a bit. I'm always praying that the engine won't stall when I go to turn it back on.... One of my worst crashes was in 1912 near Shamokin, when I tried to go over a culm bank at the Cameron Colliery."

"What's culm?" I wonder.

"Culm is the waste left over after anthracite coal mining, made out of coal dust and dirt. That mountain of culm was around 2,000 feet high—the highest in the world!"

"You were awfully brave!"

"Ha! I guess so. Brave and crazy. Daring, if you will. They called me the Birdman back then. I just kept trying. Nothing could stop me from flying."

"So what happened next?"

"One of those pesky wind gusts. It's especially hard to control an aeroplane in the mountains around here. The wind is unpredictable at best. So down I went, dropping about one hundred feet, and turning upside down! I was pinned under the plane. People came running, figuring I was probably dead, but I sure surprised them! I'll admit I wasn't feeling all that chipper, though. But, once I got out of the hospital, I was even more determined to improve upon those early pushers, so they'd be easier to control in a gust."

"What's a pusher?"

"It's a biplane that has the propeller in the back instead of the front, like this plane does."

"Did you fix it?"

"Yes I did, at least I made it better, and my next big public exhibition was in 1914, right across the Susquehanna River at Rolling Green Park. I'm headed over there now, so you can see."

"But aren't we in a hurry to get back to Camden?" Oops, we really need to get back, more than he knows.

"Oh, this won't take long. It's only a few miles from here," he answers with a smile. I tap my nose three times. *Aunt Cora, can you hear me?*

Just barely, Jenna. I'm feeling a bit weaker. Are you back yet?

No. Not nearly. I'm afraid I kind of overslept. I dreamt about Aunt Alice, but I think it wasn't a dream at all, and then Uncle Emory couldn't wake me up for over an hour!

Oh Jenna. That Aunt Alice is a piece of work. I love her dearly, and she means well, but.... She told me all about your conversation.

So it really happened?

Oh yes indeed. I'm glad you got to know her, and to visit the family, but please tell Emory to step on the gas, my favorite little witch!

"And here is where they gave the Sunday afternoon concerts in the park, where I made the very first flight over Snyder County in 1914!" I hope I didn't miss too much. I just realized that Uncle Emory is talking to me…. I look down and see a big amusement park, crowded with lots of happy Fourth of July revelers. I can hear the music from the merry-go-round. We're flying awfully close to the Ferris wheel….

"They were all sitting outside on those benches, right over there, waiting for the concert to begin, when *ROAR!* I came flying up over their heads in my pusher. You should have seen their faces! They had never seen an airplane before, and I was flying real low, so you just know it was deafeningly loud."

"They never forgot *that* concert, say Uncle Emory?" I laugh. I look down and see everyone looking up at us again today, mouths open, fingers pointing. Aviation is still pretty young in 1926, and seeing an airplane flying overhead still isn't a humdrum, everyday occurrence.

"You know," he adds, "I could do some swoops and turns and figure eights and drum up plenty of customers right here today! Do you feel like doing a little barnstorming, Jenna?" he asks with a naughty grin.

"I would love to, Uncle Emory," I say, thinking fast, "but I promised Aunt Cora I'd be back early. I know she's waiting for me right now, and she has plans for today!"

"Aw, ok, you're right for sure, Jenna," he says, sounding disappointed. My uncle sure loves to fly, and that's a fact. "So now we'll head south through Selinsgrove, then to Harrisburg, then over east toward Philly and Camden. We should be there in about two hours, I'd say." I'm feeling relieved, and hoping that all will be well. I take a big bite of cornbread, and hold on tight to the rest, so it won't blow away. Flying cornbread crumbs, a new Fourth of July tradition!

"Look down now, Jenna! There's Selinsgrove!" I know that's where Buckadee grew up, and where her dad, Warren, grew up too. "I was the very first to fly over this town, back in 1914, soon after my flight over Rolling Green Park. They closed down all the factories and other businesses, so people could watch."

"You made history, you know, Uncle Birdman."

"I suppose you're right, my Jenna. And I'm mighty proud of that, indeed!"

23. A Bit of a Glitch

"Trumpets and drums and John Philip Sousa!" I laugh out loud.

"*Stars and Stripes Forever.* 'Tis the Fourth of July for sure!" sings out Uncle Emory, flying low over the parade in Selinsgrove. "Right over there, on Market Street, I met your cousin Wilfred, Annie's son." Ok, Wilfred was actually my great-great uncle, but I won't mention that.

"Tell me more!" I say, knowing the story by heart.

"Well, a couple of days after my famous flight over Selinsgrove, I decided to fly over the town again, and check out my sister Annie's new house." Annie was actually my great-great grandmother. Her son Warren was my Buckadee's daddy and my mom's "Pappy."

"Did you see it?" I ask.

"Well, I didn't quite make it that far south, because I ran into a bit of a glitch. In spite of the improvements I had made to my aeroplane, a tricky little breeze managed to tip my wings just enough to knock me off course, right down into the electrical wires, and I crashed on the road, right over there." The band is marching right where he's pointing. "Fortunately, the roads weren't paved back then, or it would have been worse. But all the power was knocked out—all the way to Sunbury!"

"And that's when you met Wilfred?" I egg him on.

"Yes. All the little school kiddies came running over to see what happened, and little Will was the first on the scene. I recognized him, but he didn't know me from Adam."

"Then what?"

"Well, I was in pretty bad shape, having just fallen out of the sky, but I was still conscious enough to say, 'Hey, little boy! You look like you could be my nephew! What's your name?' Well, let me tell you—he hightailed it out of there like he had seen a ghost! Ha! And that's the last thing I remember until I woke up in Dr. Decker's office an hour or so later."

"Look, Uncle Emory, someone's waving at us!"

"Oh my gosh, speak of the devil! That's my sister Annie Groce right now, standing on her front porch! And there are two young men standing next to her. Wait, that would be Warren and Wilfred, all grown up!"

I'm waving with all my might at my great grandfather Warren, my great-great uncle Wilfred, and my great-great grandmother Annie. My mind is officially blown!

"Oh my, Jenna, I haven't seen my sister for some time. I'll have to fly back up in the fall, after the Sesqui is over, and have a good visit with her, if she'll have me. She still isn't comfortable sharing me with her whiter side of the family. What a sad state of affairs. Maybe I'll just send her another letter, and leave it at that."

"How horrible, Uncle Emory, that we live in a world where sisters and brothers stay away from each other because of fear, because we live in such a divided society."

"You're right, Jenna, it is indeed because of fear. Annie's afraid of how she'd be treated by her neighbors, including local Klan members, if they knew she was African American by birth, plus we have some Native American blood as well, I've been told. So if she introduces me as her brother, and they see that I'm black, then the cat's out of the bag, and she and her husband and children are potentially in danger."

"When you think about it, Uncle Emory, we humans probably all have mixed heritage, when you go back enough generations. I wonder why we're all pitted against each other like we are?"

"Follow the money," he answers. Hmm, I heard that same expression coming from GB not so long ago.... "Yup," he continues, "it brings to mind that old expression, 'divide and conquer.' If you pit people against each other for petty reasons, like race or sex or religion or sexual orientation, and make them afraid of each other, then they won't notice how they're all being manipulated and taken advantage of by the same folks who are running the show. If we all saw each other as one big loving family, think of the possibilities!"

"Gosh!" I laugh, imagining a happier world. "But now it's set up like in the Wizard of Oz, when the man behind the curtain, who's trying to scare Dorothy and her friends, says, 'Don't pay any attention to the man behind the curtain!'"

"Yes!" agrees Uncle Emory. "I hear they made a Broadway play out of the book." Oops, but they didn't make the movie until 1939....

———

"Speaking of curtains, what in the world is *that?*" I ask, alarmed. "Do you see it, Uncle Emory? Right up ahead. It looks like a curtain of rainbows!" Our bright sunny day is about to be intercepted by a magical mist that extends from the river to as high as the eye can see. We've been flying south toward Harrisburg above the Susquehanna River, but suddenly, *poof!* the whole landscape disappears.

"Oh NO-O-O!" he shouts, as the curtain closes over us. We're surrounded by a white mist, infused with tiny rainbow droplets glimmering all around us.

"Oh, how beautiful!" I exclaim, even though I'm scared to death.

"I've never encountered such a fog!" says Uncle Emory. I turn around to look at him, but he's disappeared too! "Hold on Jenna," he instructs me. "I'll turn the plane around and head back out of this mess." He banks the biplane hard, then accelerates north. We should be back in the sunshine by now, but we're not. We keep flying and flying, but we're still entrenched within the enchanted mist. I'm softly singing, *the colors of the rainbow, so pretty in the sky,* but it's not cheering me up.

"Oh me oh my. Well, we can't fly out of it, but maybe we can fly over it," Uncle Emory says with a shaky voice as we climb upward. And climb. And climb. And climb. No luck whatsoever, and it's getting mighty cold up here. I can see tiny ice particles sparkling on the tip of my nose, and it's kind of hard to breathe.

"Well, that sure didn't work out, now did it?" gasps my uncle. "I'll take us down again quickly, before the engine freezes up, and turn back south toward Harrisburg. At least I can see my compass. I'm hoping we're still over the Susquehanna River, so we can avoid all the mountains and the coal region to the east."

"Good idea. I sure wouldn't want to encounter that giant culm bank today!" I shiver at the thought of being permanently embedded inside a mountain of coal dust. And now the wind's picking up. A lot.

"I'm scared, Uncle Emory!"

"I wish I could tell you everything's just fine, but…I'm scared too," he admits. I tap my nose three times. I wait a bit then tap it three more times. Nothing. *Nada.*

After a little while, Uncle Emory says, "We should be at least as far as Harrisburg by now, so I'll ease over toward the southeast. Hopefully, we're heading more or less directly for Philadelphia." It seems like we've been flying forever. The mist is still as dense as ever, and now there seems to be a greenish luster in addition to the shimmering rainbows. Hmm. Methinks there's magic afoot. I tap my nose three more times.

Oh Jenna, I'm so sorry!

Aunt Cora?

No, it's me, Alice.

Aunt Alice?

Yes. I got to worrying about you getting back to Cora on time, so I decided to send a nice little breeze, to, you know, help you on your way. But it looks like my spell isn't working as planned, is it?

What? You sent this glittery magical mist instead of a breeze? We can't see a thing!

I tried to do the thing I thought I could not do, but...I really couldn't!

"We're getting low on gas, and we still can't see a thing." Uncle Emory sounds despondent. Once again I look up, down, all around, then down again.

"I think I see something!" I shout. "It looks like a thin dark line down below." I turn around, and I can actually see Uncle Emory's face!

"Yes!" he hollers, laughing for joy. "It's the Pennsylvania Railroad tracks! Jenna, you've saved the day! You're my hero! We can follow them right into Philly!" He starts bringing the plane down lower, now that he knows we're not about to smash into a mountain.

"AAHHH!" I scream.

"What happened?"

"Something just brushed right against my head, and scared the bejeepers out of me!"

Uncle Emory squints at me through his goggles. "Well, look at that! You've just received a message that we're close to home—you have a white New Jersey seagull feather stuck in your hair!"

"Whoo Hoo!" we both shout for joy. Gosh, just a few curls sticking out from my helmet, and a fashion-conscious seagull goes and sticks a feather in them—and am I ever grateful!

Now the mist is lifting even more, and we can see the sun setting behind us...bright vermillion and gold, with streaks of magenta, and a border of dusty rose...periwinkle blue just beyond, fading into dusk. And there's Philadelphia up ahead, glowing a pink gold, with Camden and her glistening Nipper building just beyond. What a beautiful relief to know where we are!

I tap my nose three times. Silence. I try again.

Meow! I hear faintly.

Glinda! Where's Aunt Cora? I hear a faint moan. A human one.

Aunt Cora! I hear you! I'm almost home! As we approach the city, I notice that the sunset is fading quickly. Now it's almost dark.

Jenna! You need to be here now! Her voice is so soft, I can hardly hear it at all.

What can I do?

Tap your nose three times, while thinking of Glinda and me, and picturing yourself in my home.

I tap my nose three times. Nothing happens. Suddenly I'm surrounded by bright golden lights!

"Oh no! The fireworks have begun over the Delaware River!" laughs Uncle Emory. "And we're right in the middle of them!" He veers the plane to the left, so we're not directly over them, but not before another blast of color starts bursting all around us. Red, white, and blue. Wow!

I can see the colors through your eyes! Aunt Cora sounds a little stronger. *Now Jenna, try again, only harder.*

OK. I close my eyes tight, tap my nose three times, and picture myself in the room with Aunt Cora and Glinda, and meditating on how much I love them. I envision this with all my might, when suddenly, *POOF!* I feel myself somersaulting through the air, and see spectacular fireworks in rainbow colors all around me, even though my eyes are still closed.

Goodbye, Jenna, I hear a deeper voice.

What?

It's your Uncle Emory.

You knew all along?

Yes and no. I figured, with Cora in the picture, that some kind of enchantment was afoot. I'm a Malick from Winnengen too, you know.

Of course! And that would help explain how you survived all those...gravitational challenges, and how you managed to rise above all the prejudices and follow your dream, and make history. I love you, Uncle Emory. You're my hero. Thank you for our time together. And please continue to be the best possible aviator, and please...watch your back.

I will. I'm aware of the challenges—and of the dangers—of gravity combined with bigotry, but I choose to keep on keeping on. I'd rather give life my best shot, instead of sitting on the ground and wishing I were above it! I'll fly as long as I possibly can.

Please consider staying home on May 20, 1928.

I will take your advice under consideration. I know that you are wise beyond your years. Although I suspect that many other nine-year-olds are wise too, but nobody pays any attention.

—

94

That's for sure, Uncle Emory!

And thank you, Jenna. You're my hero too. We make quite a team! I love you.

I love you.

Thud. I suddenly find myself landing heavily on my feet right in front of Aunt Cora's apartment. Thank goodness for these heavy aviator's boots! I brush myself off, and reach out to touch the door. It swings open, just like last time. But this time there's no music, and the light is so low I can hardly see. I feel a very bony Glinda rubbing against my legs, as I look around.

There she is. Or is it Aunt Alice? Over on the sofa lies a very old woman, glowing green, with silver curls and a deeply lined face. I run over and kneel by her side.

"Aunt Cora, it's you! I'm here! Please be OK!"

"Jenna," she smiles weakly. "Just look at you! Goodness, what's that in your hair?"

"That's my souvenir from Aunt Alice's magical mist! A seagull gave it to me, to let us know we were close to home."

"Ha! Didn't I tell you? That Aunt Alice is a piece of work!" Aunt Cora sounds a little stronger. Laughter is good medicine, you know. "Now, take my hand, dear. Let's get you back to your grandmas, then Glinda and I will be OK. I'm afraid I've been keeping the magic going a little too long!"

"Thank you for this amazing journey, Aunt Cora. I'll miss you." I kiss her cheek gently.

"Oh, I'll miss you too, my Jenna! Thank you too! You've brought such joy to my life. What an incredible couple of days!"

I grasp her hand in mine, and look at her beloved, albeit green, face. Her wart has grown bigger and longer, practically hiding her nose underneath its weight.

"OK," she instructs. "Let's see what we can do." We hold hands tightly, and she says, "Jenna, picture yourself near the freight elevator door on the first floor, right here in the Nipper building, in the year 2016." We both concentrate really hard and tap our noses three times. Her giant wart wobbles.

Nada.

"You know, Aunt Cora, part of me really wants to stay right here with you, so maybe I'm not wishing hard enough."

"True, Jenna. Same for me. But we'll always be together now, no matter what. Just tap your nose three times, and I'll be with you. After all, you're my sister Witch of Winnengen!"

"What does that mean, exactly?" I ask.

"Well, Jenna," she pauses to think. "It means what you want it to mean. So, what would you like it to mean?"

OK, that threw me for a loop! I expected…what, an instruction manual? "Gosh, I don't quite know, Aunt Cora. I guess I'll have to figure it out as I go along. I do know that I've learned a lot over the course of this awesome visit, and I'd like to share what I've learned with others. I've learned that it's important to know our history, and I don't just mean the stuff we learn in school! How many students learn about Uncle Emory, or Julia Clarke, or the Feltons, or Charles Wesley Peters, or Mamie Smith? Or Geraldine Farrar? Or you, Aunt Cora? Or the Witches of Winnengen? I think maybe I'll research unknown history—those stories that are still hidden away, and I'll write, and teach. That way I'll help empower other nine-year-old girls, and everyone else besides."

"That's powerful magic indeed, my dear!"

"Yes, Aunt Cora. I feel more self-confident now, knowing that there were so many women and black pilots, singers, movers and shakers. And I've learned so much about my own family, and about life in 1926, and about the fabulous city of Camden. My world has shifted quite a bit since I met you, Aunt Cora, and I feel like I have an important place in it. More important than I realized."

"Aunt Alice and Uncle Emory and I were all correct about you, my dear Jenna. You are indeed a wise child! OK," she continues, "I have an idea. Help me to sit up, please." I reach behind her shoulders, and lift her up, swinging her legs around to the front. She's so light, she practically levitates! Glinda jumps up on her lap, and I pat her as I sit down next to Aunt Cora on the green velvet sofa. Glinda still feels soft and airy, but looks so thin and old, like my aunt. I hope they'll both be alright. Uh oh, I'm starting to cry.

"We'll be OK, dear," says Aunt Cora, her eyes welling with tears. "I love you too, Jenna. Now, let's do this!"

We both tap our noses and hold hands, with our other hands touching Glinda. I think about how much love I've felt on this journey, and then I think about all the love I feel for my grandmothers, who will soon emerge from the elevator, expecting me to be there!

Whoosh!

Where am I? I look around and see that I'm on the bottom of a ramp in a passageway that looks kind of like the stairwells inside the Nipper building, with the same white concrete and brick walls. There's a trash can, and someone's resting on a folding chair, drinking from a bottle of iced tea, reading a magazine, and wearing a white apron. Now wait, I know him! It's the guy who runs the deli downstairs!

"Hi!" I say. He jumps, drops the magazine, and looks around.

"What in the world are you doing here, young lady?" He looks like he's seen a ghost. I look down to see if I'm still dressed like Queen Bess, but I'm wearing the same jeans and T-shirt I had on when my adventure began. Then it dawns on me that the ramp that I'm on is walled off behind me. In other words, there's really no logical way that I could actually be standing here....

"I was just looking for the freight elevator," I say in a small voice.

"Ah! OK. Just follow me," he says, shaking his head in confusion as he leads me into the deli and around past the cold cuts, through the kitchen, and out a door into the back hallway. I follow him around a corner, down another hallway, and through a set of gray double doors. Then he points me over past the loading dock and right there to the elevator. I arrive just as the door opens.

"You beat us!" says Buckadee sternly. "You must have been running at breakneck speed down all those steps, you naughty girl, you!" I run over and give her the biggest hug ever, then turn to hug Grandma Butch.

"Whoa! What just tickled my nose?" asks GB.

"Oh my goodness gracious!" exclaims Buckadee. I'm going to complain to management that they have birds in the stairwells! You have a large white feather in your hair, Jenna!"

"Buckadee, you never met Aunt Cora, right?" I ask, and then take another bite of my grilled cheese and tomato.

"No, of course not, dear. She died of the Spanish flu in 1918 and I wasn't born till 1950!" Buckadee takes another sip of her Arnold Palmer. "But, I must say, ever since I found her picture in my grandmother's attic, I've been intrigued by her. She looks so strong, yet so kind and gentle. I'm sure I would have loved her dearly; in fact, I do, indeed, love her dearly, just like I love her brother Emory and her sister Laura, and I never met them either."

"How about Aunt Alice?" I continue between bites. I look out the Pub window. Hey, it's not raining! Then I look over at the Ben Franklin Bridge and imagine being on it again with Geraldine Farrar and Aunt Cora, and then actually flying over it in Uncle Emory's airplane!

"I would have loved to have met Aunt Alice too. She died in 1926...July 10."

"What from?"

"Dementia." Gulp. So it's all true. Buckadee continues, "Emory and Laura were both close to Alice, and are buried right next to her in Wolf's Crossroads Cemetery right outside of Sunbury. I don't know how well Cora and Annie knew her, since they were both adopted by other families after their mother died of typhoid in 1887. Why do you ask, dear?"

"Family. It's important, don't you think?"

"Oh yes, I'm with you on that! And there are so many family members that I never even knew we had until fairly recently, so now I want to make up for lost time by learning whatever I can about them. Sometimes I even pretend to talk to them, even though they couldn't possibly hear me...or could they?" she wonders aloud as she harpoons another chunk of cucumber and pops it in her mouth.

"Grandma Butch?"

"Yes, Sunshine?" she asks, as she rips into her burger.

"I've made up my mind!" I announce.

She studies my face as she finishes chewing, then swallows. "About what?"

"I'd be glad to be your assistant and answer any questions people might have about the Victor Talking Machine Company, the city of Camden, and your awesome painting of the futuristic Camden WaterWalk."

"You've already decided, and we haven't even had dessert yet?" GB looks bemused. "You must have done some serious soul searching on your way down those stairs...you weren't the least bit interested when I asked you an hour ago!"

I just smile and take another bite of my sandwich.

"Oh my!" exclaims Buckadee, looking at her watch. "I'd better get back upstairs *pronto* and transform into Geraldine Farrar—the time's getting away from me!"

"They'll have refreshments at the Nipper Fest, right?" I ask. GB nods. "Well then, let's all go up and get ready. We can have dessert later."

"This is a day of miracles," laughs GB as we head on out.

"It sure is!" I agree. We take the main elevator up to the fifth floor. I'm not quite ready for the stairs again so soon. Next time.

As soon as we walk into the apartment, Buckadee runs toward her closet, so the transformation can begin, and Grandma Butch heads to her comfortable chair in the bedroom. I walk slowly across the living room toward the sofa, the events of the last two days—or was it just two hours?—swirling around in my brain.

No, it couldn't be! Darned if Daphne the mannequin didn't just wink at me!

"There is a lady, sweet and kind,
was never face so pleas'd my mind.
I did but see her passing by,
and yet I love her till I die."

After the clapping subsides, I walk over to her. "Buckadee, I love that song! Did you just learn it?"

"Oh, no, dear. I've known this song forever. In fact, I remember hearing it for the first time when I was just your age!" she smiles, then looks closer. "Jenna, I love your outfit! I see you've incorporated your white feather...."

"Yup!" I say proudly. "Notice that I'm also wearing that flapper costume of yours that was hanging in the closet. You were too busy to ask, but GB said it'd be OK. She helped me find a sash, so the hem wouldn't drag on the floor. Guess who I am?"

"Hmm," she concentrates, looking closely. "Bessie Smith?"

"Close, but no cigar!" I say with a smug grin. "I'm Mamie Smith, the First Lady of the Blues, and she recorded right here for the Victor Talking Machine Company in 1926!"

"Wow! I didn't know that! You're something else, Ms. Jenna!" I bow and back away, so she can continue with her performance.

"MAMIE SMITH, EVERYBODY!" she announces loudly. "The young lady passing by is the First Lady of the Blues, and she recorded right here for Victor in 1926!" They all laugh and applaud, as I take a gracious bow. I look around the Caruso Room and see some familiar faces, including the poet and teacher Mr. Rocky, who's dressed up as Walt Whitman. He sees me and instantly produces his puppet Bongo, who waves happily, bouncing from side to side. Then I see the artist William Butler and his wife Ronja, who have done so much for the arts here in Camden. Their gallery is right down the street. And there's Ms. Angela, another poet and neighbor, who creates beautiful photo books about Camden. I love her smile. And over there is Ms. Cassie, who just opened an art gallery, the FireWorks, over in South Camden, and Mr. Perks, the President of the Camden County Historical Society, who will be

singing and playing his guitar as soon as Buckadee is done with her set. And there's Mr. Barnum, who wrote the book about the Victor Talking Machine Company. Look! Isn't that the Broadway star, Graham Alexander? He plans to open a museum in Building #2, and it will be all about the history of recorded music—which began right here in Camden. This city is amazing! I wave to them all as I tiptoe out the door and into the courtyard, where the art show is being held.

The harp music is filling the air with magic, as I cross over to Grandma Butch and her painting. First I stop to say hi to Ms. Liesl, who organized this whole exhibit. She's sitting beside her beautiful cards and photographs. Liesl has to stay in a wheelchair because she has MS, but she does more for the arts here in Camden than a dozen people who can walk around!

"Grandma Butch, that is such a cool painting!"

"Just look at you, Jenna!" she beams. "I swear, you're the belle of the ball!"

"Ha!" I laugh and curtsy to her as a couple of people walk over and ask me about Mamie Smith. I also tell them about Geraldine Farrar and, in fact, all the singers and musicians I met...just earlier today, when I visited Camden in 1926. *Cheesh.*

"GB, is it OK if I walk across the street to Building #2? I want to see the auditorium on the eighth floor, and Mr. Johnson's office on the seventh. They're open to the public today for the Nipper Fest, right?" I ask.

"Yes, indeed, dear. They're even giving tours. I'd better stay here with the exhibit, but tell me what it's like! Maybe I can get over there later."

This day is so perfect. The rain is gone, the air is fresh, and there's not a cloud in the sky. Johnson Park is also part of the festivities, since the Johnson Library, now the Walt Whitman Art Center, is also celebrating its centennial. But right now it's pretty quiet, except for a couple of happy kiddies running around. Most of the people are over on the side of the park by Building #2, where the food carts are set up. I think I'll stroll on over and visit my favorite statue. I tap my nose three times.

Well, hello there Jenna!

Aunt Cora! You sound so much better!

Meow!

And so do you, Glinda!

Yes, her fur is thicker already, and she's playing with the ribbon again. Oh Jenna, I'm learning my limitations, my dear. But expanding my capabilities every day. However, clearing up that magical mist of Alice's was almost more than I could muster!

Ha! I suspected you had a hand in that!

I was hoping to eke out one more day, so you could hear President Coolidge speak, but it would have decidedly been too much for me, and who knows what would have happened then? But check online, and you'll see that the whole event was a washout. The drenching rain didn't let up for a minute. Ha! I heard that a Camden police sergeant loaned the President his raincoat, but it was never returned!

No! How rude!

Indeed! So, I see that you're strutting your stuff there at the Nipper Fest, my darling niece. I'm so proud of you.

"Ahem!" I hear.

"Oh, Uncle Christopher! I mean, Uncle Eldridge!"

"I see you're meditating on Peter Pan."

"Yes. I love J. M. Barrie's story, and the original movie with Mary Martin!"

"Agreed—and the music is to die for." He bursts into song, *"I won't grow up!"* And I join in,

"If growing up means it would be…beneath my dignity to climb a tree,
I'll never grow up, never grow up, never grow u-up!
Not me. So there!"

"Uncle Chri…I mean, Eldridge, did you know that this Peter Pan statue was officially dedicated on September 24, 1926, when over three thousand local schoolchildren acted out scenes from the story?"

"No, I was not aware of that." His eyes are wide open under his black bowler hat. "And how, pray tell, do you always know so darn much, my dear child?"

"Because, my dear sir," I respond with a wink and a tilt of my head, "I'm a witch!"

"Jenna. I believe you," he says, shaking his handsome head, and looking eerily like the real Eldridge Johnson. "Absolutely nothing you could possibly tell me would surprise me. You're utterly fantabulous!"

At this moment, I hear the sound of a low-flying airplane.

"I'll just bet," he goes on, "you're about to tell me that the biplane flying right over our heads is being piloted by none other than Uncle Emory!"

A grin is slowly spreading from one of my ears to the other, as I look up in the sky and wave.

* * *

Emory Conrad Malick ("Uncle Emory") was, in fact, our first licensed black pilot, the first aviator to fly over central Pennsylvania, the first African American pilot to earn a Federal Transport License, a "barnstormer," and a pioneer in aerial photography.

During his trip back to New Jersey with a new airplane for his 1926 promotion, "See the Sesqui by Air," Uncle Emory had a scary adventure. According to the *Mount Carmel Item*, "Between Uniontown and Chambersburg he encountered a dense fog and lost his bearings. Relying upon his compass he flew back to Harrisburg and then worked his way to Philadelphia following the railroad tracks."

Emory's youngest sister, Cora, died from the Spanish flu pandemic in 1918, along with her husband and three young daughters. Emory's and Cora's sister Laura lived for a time in Sunbury with their Aunt Alice Malick. Aunt Alice worked as a servant and housemaid, and she died on July 10, 1926, of dementia. Cora's, Laura's, and Emory's sister Annie Groce was the author's paternal grandmother. The whole family is descended from the Moelichs of Winnengen, Germany.

The author, Mary Groce, lives with her partner Susan Atlas in the Victor Lofts, also known as the Nipper Building, which was Building #17 of the Victor Talking Machine Company in Camden, New Jersey, the birthplace of the recording industry.

The Nipper Fest, celebrating the centennial of the Nipper Building, Building #2, and the Walt Whitman Art Center, was held on September 10, 2016.

Made in the USA
Lexington, KY
10 May 2018